When An Alien Moves In Next Door

Part One of The Slurpinthal Series

K.S. Riggin

Table of Contents

Chapter One:

The Night He Came

Slurpinthal. The name sounded almost like a frozen drink or the sound of a place you're not really sure you want to visit. It could have been someone's name — an uncle I'd never met or the last name of a general in the United States Army, a football player, even a strange instrument . . . Slurpinthal could have been a lot of things, but not anyone or anything you might guess. I promise you that.

On Friday, he moved next to us — next door to the house where I lived with my mom, dad, my sister Clara, and, sometimes, a flea-bitten, scrawny cat named Marbles. He was a tuxedo cat with short hair and had a crooked tail. Instead of having a curve like most cats, Marbles had a twist at the top, so he always waved his tail looking like a backwards question mark.

Marbles wasn't really ours, but he liked to hang out in our backyard, probably because Dad kept putting out food for him, hoping to catch him. Marbles was too wily for cages. He was feral, so we weren't allowed to attempt to pet him. That's what Mom always said, but, Clara and I liked having a cat, even if it was only part time and one we couldn't touch.

But, back to Slurpinthal, our new neighbor. He took up residence during the middle of the night, which I think was rather suspicious in itself. But the way he did it was even more bizarre. I saw no moving van, and he didn't lug in any heavy furniture. He was alone, too. He didn't have a wife or kids, like everyone else in our cul-de-sac, and if

1

he had any pets, they must have been the size of a goldfish or a hermit crab.

I think that was really strange because the house at the end of the street was the biggest house in the whole neighborhood. We used to call it the Simon's house, because a long time ago a family of that name lived there. They left when I was three, so I hardly remember them. But Dad said that the house had at least five bedrooms, a huge family room, a living room, and even a rec room, where the Simons had set up a pool table, which was how Dad knew about the house, since he used to play pool with Mr. Simon.

My name is Kyle, and I was born here in Riverton —not in our house, but in the local hospital. Mom and Dad have lived here even longer. They inherited our four bedrooms, two baths, with a family room/den from my grandparents, Dad's parents. It was a pretty cool house with a great backyard and a garage where we kept our bikes. Well, mine was still there, but I couldn't ride it anymore.

I'm eleven, a sixth grader this year. Next year, I'll be going to the new junior high where all the mean kids go. Sometimes I wished we didn't have to keep getting older. You know what I mean? Like, maybe we could stop and wait a while until we were really ready to rearrange our lives into new schools, new surroundings, or being at the same place as all the tough guys who hung out at junior high.

Todd, my best friend, liked being a big shot at the elementary school, but he said it would be no problem to jump over to junior high. His dad was a cop. Maybe that's why Todd always felt so secure. My dad was just a veterinarian who fixed up cows and horses with stomach problems. My father never understood about mean kids. He said, "If you're tough enough to slip a tube down a horse's nose, you shouldn't have any trouble with bullies."

"Sure, Dad," I always responded, nodding like I agreed with him. I mean, a horse could bite your arm if you were too slow, but it didn't wait for you down at the end of the street, ready to tip over your wheelchair and . . .

Oops. I meant to tell you about Slurpinthal, and now I've led you down to the creek bed. Sorry about that. It's a bad habit I have. My teacher said that I need to stop at the end of each paragraph and take a long, deep breath. I try, but that usually doesn't work for me. Stuff just all comes gurgling out.

Anyway, when it happened, I mean about Mr. Slurpinthal moving in . . .

Dad said he was glad someone had finally decided to live in the empty house. He said it made people think our neighborhood was undesirable when a house stayed empty. Undesirable, a word that tickled your tongue, it was so interesting, but it couldn't be used in school. Multi-syllabic words almost always got you in trouble with your peers. I learned that the hard way. (I like to collect words, though. You never know when you might be able to dust one off and make use of it. At least, someday.)

Dad never had to worry about guarding his vocabulary. Horses and cows never objected to big words. They never . . .

It wasn't a bad neighborhood where we live. There were always lots of kids playing in the cul-de-sac. You could find a great baseball game going on every Saturday right in front of our house because our street formed a big round area, one that was perfect for all the bases.

I watched all the games, even though I couldn't play. I wondered if Mr. Slurpinthal liked baseball. Maybe he'd tell the kids they couldn't play there anymore. I hoped he wouldn't do that. Some of the kids were nicer to me because of the baseball field that's practically in my front yard.

But I was telling you about the night Slurpinthal moved in. You see, no one heard anything. It was as quiet as any other night. I mean, you could hear the crickets whistling their legs together. Down at the pond, a couple of bullfrogs usually spent their nights singing to their lady friends. They were not very musical, only competitive, trying to see which one had the deepest and loudest frog bellow.

You couldn't actually see the Spit-and-Wallow Pond from here, but you could always hear it. Mom said the frogs kept her up at night; they were so loud, but I think she was kidding. I hardly ever heard them, except as background noise. I didn't hear them that night, not the night when Slurpinthal arrived.

Our house was a two-story. My bedroom was on the second floor, toward the front of the house. I've got the best view of the whole cul-de-sac from my room. It let me see all the way to the elementary school on my right. Toward the left, of course, was the Simon's house — I mean, the house Slurpinthal had bought.

If I stared across the other way, I could almost make out Todd's house, even though he said I couldn't. I didn't tell him about my binoculars. He might not like the fact that I could peer into his living room anytime I wanted.

My parents paid to have an elevator installed when I came home after the accident. That was how I could get upstairs and into my bedroom. The chair lift, as it was really called, was kind of cool. My sister liked to take her friends on it. When she did, it was really funny because they always held on for dear life, as if the distance from one floor to another was that high. I guess it just seemed steeper for a preschool kid.

Mom told my sister not to use the elevator, though. I think Mom believed that one of Clara's friends might get hurt. Mom never said anything when Todd rode up with me. She just looked away and bit her lip. When Todd did take the lift up with me, he had to hold on too, but that was because he was big and had to cram himself inside to fit beside me.

The lift was pretty small, and my wheelchair took up most of the space. When Todd rode with me, he held the handgrip with only one hand to show he was cool with it. But most of the time, Todd just ran up the stairs. I wish I could. I used to.

Last time I went to see the doctor, he said I might be able to walk again someday. He'd been injecting me with a new serum, an injection that the doctors thought might grow back the feeling in my spinal cord.

Mom always cried when the doctor shoved the needle in. I always thought about the sky and the grass and how the creek chattered like a squirrel. My eyes stung because I did have some feeling in my back. But I never cried. Not until I got home, anyway.

Darn it. I was telling you about Slurpinthal. He moved in Friday night — well, actually in the dark hours of Saturday morning. I know I told you about him moving in. I told you he did it real mysteriously, too. But what I didn't tell you is that I saw something that night, something really weird.

Like I said, I can see his house perfectly from my bedroom. If I had a twenty-foot pole, I could even reach across and touch the window ledge of his upstairs bedroom. It was the one that Slurpinthal used at night. Not to sleep in. I don't think he ever slept. That light was always on.

Last Saturday, I set my alarm and checked every hour of the night. Every room was fully lit each time I looked. I figured that the guy either didn't sleep or else he was afraid of monsters.

I didn't really believe he was afraid. I decided that he was hiding out, or pretending to be something he wasn't. That was something I didn't tell anyone, not even Todd because I knew my pal wouldn't believe me.

5

You see, the night when Slurpinthal moved in, there was a light so bright in the sky that it woke me up. I sat up in my bed and looked out the window. It was a raging fire kind of light, like the sun had dropped real low and was hanging out over the neighbor's second-floor window.

Of course, I got up out of bed. I tugged my chair over, slid into it, and wheeled over to the window. I pushed the drapes back and glided the window panel to the other side. I wanted to hear what was going on as well as see.

I thought the light would make the Welches' dog bark. He always barked when he heard a strange sound — even when it wasn't that strange, like if the paperboy went riding by, or some mangy, feral cat walked across the fence waving its tail.

But that night the Welches' dog didn't bark. The crickets weren't clapping their wings, either. I think that night's silence was an *absolute* silence. That's a word my teacher, Mrs. Cordoba, just taught us. It means that what I was hearing that night was, well, the kind of silence that happens when the very lack of sound carries an ominous quality. You sense that something awful is about to take place.

I knew all about that. One time at school, my catheter started leaking, and urine was trickling down my wheelchair as I rolled along. I didn't realize it. There was just this awful silence, and then a whole school full of eyes were staring. Horror-filled eyes. Eyes like I'd turned into Dracula or something.

The hall stilled like all the kids were corpses — zombies, maybe, and then there was nothing but eyes and that *absolute silence* and me, sitting in my wheelchair with urine leaking down on the floor and puddling around my footrests.

Anyway, for some reason, I was thinking about that when I saw the light next to Slurpinthal's window. It was the same kind of shiver silence — the silence of doom. If I'd had any sense, I would have slammed the window closed and wheeled myself back to bed, but just like that moment in the hall, I couldn't. I was frozen. Mummified.

The light was blinding. It hurt to look at it. My eyes were just slits as I gazed across the distance between us. And then I saw his window slowly open, but there was nobody there. Just that light.

Suddenly, the Simon's house darkened. A moment later, the light began to flicker on and off, each time brighter than before. It was throbbing, too, with a vibration of both light and sound that I could hear from the Simon's house all the way to my bedroom. It seemed as if the pulsing light was waking up the room. I don't know how the window opened. As I said, no one was there. No one until a huge ball of light blasted the dark.

As I continued to watch, something began to form inside that globe of light. It was like when the TV wasn't working well. It blinked and kind of wavered. All the dots danced up, down, and sideways. In a moment, there was a picture again, and only the memory of that oddness remained.

The window was open. The ball of light was glowing, and the inside area grew less fuzzy. The dots gathered themselves into a shape, and that shape turned into a man.

I know what you're thinking — that I was just dreaming all this. But I wasn't. The breeze through the window was making me shiver. I had goosebumps marching up and down in a line across my arms. My feet felt like ice cubes were attached to my toes. Believe me, I was awake.

And later, after I'd crawled back into my bed and fallen asleep again, I found that something even weirder had happened. It was Saturday, so I'd been able to enjoy what Mom called a "lie-in." In other words, when I woke up, it was late. I sat up in bed, and the memory of what I'd seen hit me.

I touched my face — just a gesture of feeling the forehead to see if I had a fever or something, because I was feeling hot and sweaty. My hand on my forehead made me cry out. The touch of my fingers burned me.

I got out of bed and slid into my wheelchair. I wasn't too coherent at that moment, I didn't think about the pain of my fingers touching my forehead. I just pushed on the wheels, and headed for the bathroom. I didn't intend to eye myself in the mirror. I've never been vain, even before the accident.

But as I traveled past the mirror, I caught a glance and let out a shriek. Luckily, my vocal chords weren't working yet that day, or I would have frightened my sister and parents. I did that later when I arrived downstairs when they saw me. You see, I'd turned into a lobster boy!

Now I know I've skipped over some parts in the story. I had to. You see, you wouldn't have believed me otherwise. What proof did I have of what I'd seen that night? But I had proof, all right. It was the sunburn on my face and across my bare-skinned arms. I was cherry red, tomato red, second-degree burn red.

Remember that bright light? Remember how I sat there with my head and arms dangling out the window? You can't get sunburned at two o'clock in the morning — not when the sun has set and the sky is darker than the new asphalt on the school's parking lot.

The memory made me shiver in spite of my burns. It reminded me of how at the end of the bright light fading into a body, the man's eyes had stared into mine. The distance between us had been short, and it was like he'd tried to vacuum me up into his vision. My hands had grabbed the chair's handrails. I'd fought to stay in the chair. The pull of those eyes had been that forceful. And then, he'd blinked.

I was free then, free to back away, to slam the window shut, to hurl myself across the room to my bed, scarcely feeling the mighty heave as I flung my body across the sheets. I'd cowered, blankets over my head, shuddering and worrying that the strange light might float across and rap at my window, demanding something awful, but it hadn't. Apparently, the man had just climbed through his window and taken up residence.

So I've written this down just in case something happened to me. You see, I know too much. I know about Slurpinthal. I don't think he belongs here.

You probably still don't believe me. Ask my doctor. My mother took me to see him Saturday morning, even though normally Dr. Karoni didn't do office visits on Saturdays. He did it that day for me and for my mom.

Dr. Karoni looked me over and then prescribed something for my skin. I'm sure you could see the proof of that in his medical notes. The doctor had to have wondered what would turn a white boy red in the middle of the night. I wish I knew what he wrote in my medical folder.

Meanwhile, I went upstairs later and jotted everything down. I figured it might be wise to keep a journal of all the things I'd observed. Maybe someday a scientist would thank me for my research. But no matter what, I knew that nothing would ever feel the same again. It had all slipped into *different* as if life were a kaleidoscope of shifting colors and images, because, you see, the real and the unreal had just kind of slid into each other.

Maybe that didn't make sense, but what I was trying to say is that Slurpinthal was not just a normal neighbor. If I'm right, if everything I saw really happened, and I'm sure that it did. I think, impossible as it seemed, I was pretty sure that the truth was that Slurpinthal was an extraterrestrial. Yeah, I mean that. An E.T. A real, *alien from outer space*.

Chapter Two:

The Right Thing To Do

On Sunday, my parents decided it was time to rush over and greet the new neighbor. My folks said that I had to go with them because Dad thought "it was the right thing to do." He was very big on that expression. I got a dose of it almost daily.

How did someone know what was *right*? Was it right for an alien to move in next door? What if the alien was scheming to take over the world? Maybe he was the lead explorer for more aliens? What if he was planning to fly that huge bulb of light over to our window some night and insert himself inside my father or me? There was a good chance that he might want to murder me just to keep me from telling what I knew.

But of course I didn't say any of that to Dad. I hadn't told anyone what I saw. I couldn't. You know what they'd say. Mom would probably send me off to bed, like I was five years old or something. Then she'd take my temperature and call up Dr. Karoni to see if I was having a reaction to one of the drugs I was taking.

Mom thought everything was a reaction. If I didn't drink my milk one day, that must be a reaction. If I was tired, late for breakfast, had a fight with my sister, or if the wheelchair got turned over by one of the junior high thugs, Mom thought it was a bad reaction to my medicines — even though I'd told her over and over that none of those things were related.

Anyway, that's what she'd say if I explained about what I saw on Friday night. "You're having another bad reaction," she'd tell me, her hand on my forehead as if that were the true indicator of such things.

That's was just what Mom had said about the burns on my face and arms — a bad reaction to meds. I knew the burns weren't connected to any drugs Dr. Karoni had given me. I remembered too clearly all that I saw — the light, the window opening by itself, and that awful transformation happening in the bubble I saw floating next to that second-story bedroom.

I shivered each time I thought about that and the way the man's eyes tried to pull me out of the window. Would I have fallen down onto the pavement below? Would I be dead if the alien had gotten his way? Or would the alien have scooped me up into the light to carry me off to another world? What if he hadn't blinked?

If I told my parents what I saw, Dad would give me that *look*, the one that traveled up and down my spine like a CAT scan, buzzing as it checked each vital organ. That was the same watchful appraisal he used when he checked over every horse or a cow. It was like he was an X-ray machine that could see deep inside. The funny thing was that it worked for knowing what was wrong with animals.

Once, when I went with Dad out to Cornstock's Farm, the owner brought out his favorite riding horse. The animal looked just fine to me. It was neighing loudly, picking up its hooves, and kind of dancing like horses do when they're scared. I didn't notice the way its tail was slightly thinned or how its coat didn't have the exact sheen of the other horses out in the meadow, but Dad did. He pointed those things out to me, just after he used that look of his and saw right inside the gelding. My father knew with that glance of his that Mr. Cornstock's horse had worms — without running a single test.

My father was a great vet. He has always been super good with animals, but not so much with people. Dad believed everyone was a good person deep inside, but Dad's X-ray eyes really failed him there.

One day, Dad and I were walking over to the grocery store to pick up some milk when we passed Tom Sumpers. The thug leered at me like he always did, but Dad didn't see that. Dad smiled back at the creep, and then my father told me later that Tom had kind eyes.

I knew Tom Sumpers a lot better than Dad. Tom was not the least bit kind. He was a total jerk. Everyone at school knew that. Everyone who met him could figure that out in a couple of minutes, Except my father. I guess Dad's eyes could only see things like worms or digestive problems. His X-ray vision didn't catch cruel streaks, like when a person thinks it's okay to taunt a kid and tip over his wheelchair just to watch him crawl.

I could have told my sister Clara about the alien. She would have believed me. She was okay. But my little sister had nightmares and was scared of the dark. Sometimes I had to go in and read to her when she woke up. She was always crying and hugging her doll like that was going to save her from night monsters.

Mom and Dad don't realize that. Oh, they knew Clara had to have a nightlight on, or she wouldn't go to bed. They saw that sometimes my sister had dark shadows under her eyes, like she hadn't gotten enough sleep. Mom thought she could fix all that. She told Clara not to watch scary movies. But Clara would never watch anything creepy. Lately, Clara got scared even watching cartoons.

The day my parents demanded that we go next door to see the new neighbor, Clara blanket-wrapped Babydoll for our visit. Babydoll was Clara's oldest doll, the one with only one eyelash because Mom bought the thing — soft plastic, movable arms and legs, realistic-sized baby — at a discard store. That meant it had something wrong with it even when it was new.

13

I suppose the doll was once pretty, even with only one eyelash. Clara told me it came with clothes, too. But the doll clothes had gotten all ripped and torn from being loved. Usually, Clara tried to wrap Babydoll in cloth scraps, but they didn't stay on the doll well. It didn't matter about the state of the doll, though. My sister carried Babydoll everywhere, at least on the weekend. Mom wouldn't let her take the doll to pre-school. Mom said it would get lost or someone might pull off a leg or an arm.

I don't know if that would matter greatly. The poor thing had black smudges on its nose, ink on its legs, and a strange purple stain across its right cheek. Oh, and one leg kept popping out of the socket. I had to stick it back in about once a week.

Still, Babydoll wouldn't look too bad if it at least had some hair. I don't know what happened to the nylon fuzz it had at one time, but what was left reminded me of all the sick kids I met at the hospital when I was there, the kids going through chemotherapy.

Despite its ugliness, Babydoll managed to remain part of the family. It sat at the table in a chair. Clara pretended to feed it at every meal. Luckily, even though the doll was supposed to look realistic, its mouth didn't open. It wasn't one of those newer dolls that came with a bottle and wet itself when you gave it water.

I'm glad of that, since sometimes Babydoll mysteriously climbed into my backpack. Tom Sumpers caught me with it one time. That's why he hated me so much. I tried to explain about Clara and the way she always put it in my backpack when she wanted me to fix the doll's leg, but none of that mattered to Tom. He said it was dumb for a sixth-grade boy to have a doll in his backpack. Tom Sumpers said it turned me into a sissy.

That was the first time Tom turned over my wheelchair. He did it real gentle, careful not to break anything — not that he'd care if I got hurt, but I think he figured that if the chair got wrecked, my parents would sue. I don't think they would. My folks don't think like that. Dad would probably just ask Tom to come and help him out with his vet checks. I bet Dad would make Tom push in the worm tube on a horse.

That's the kind of stuff I used to do with Dad. I didn't do it much anymore. It was too hard for me to reach the horse's mouth. Besides, last time I tried, that's when Colonel Jim's old mare took a bite out of my arm. It's awfully hard to move back quickly when you're stuck in a chair.

I wished Tom hadn't found the doll in my backpack, but I couldn't be mad at Clara for putting it there. She had these fears, you know. That's because she saw things the rest of us didn't.

One time, she said Todd was going to get sick at the beach, and he did. Todd shouldn't have eaten three hotdogs, two caramel apples, and a bag of peanuts. I told him so, but he wouldn't listen. I didn't tell him what Clara had predicted. I wasn't supposed to tell anyone about that. It was too weird. Mom and Dad made me promise not to mention stuff like that even to my best friend.

Clara was getting better at predicting things. She said the bird's nest in the backyard, up in the Ash tree, would fall down, and it did that same day. She told me my chair had a crack, the window was going to start rattling, and that the new robot man's battery was about to stop working. She was right about all of it.

She even warned my parents about a bad storm that was going to hit during the night. Dad and Mom had just finished watching the news. I'd listened, too, because I wanted to know if the kids would be playing baseball out in the cul-de-sac that weekend. The weather forecast hadn't mentioned rain.

Since we lived near the ocean, sometimes rain showers did slip by the weathermen. On that day, Dad didn't really believe Clara, but figuring it was smart to be prepared, he went out in the dark and pushed our lawnmower back into the garage. That night, it rained enough to send puddle rivers spiraling down the driveway. The lawnmower would have been ruined.

When we got up in the morning and found the background a wall-to-wall flood, Dad and Mom should have been really grateful that Clara had warned them, but they didn't seem like they were. They went to their room and spent time doing the "serious talking" that parents do so much of.

When they finally came back into the kitchen, their faces looked all worried, like when they didn't have enough money to pay a bill and had to tell us that we wouldn't be getting our allowance for a while.

I think Mom and Dad had a talk with Clara and told her not to tell us things like that. I guess it worked for a while — until the night when Dad was explaining that his truck needed repairs, and he couldn't afford to have it fixed.

"That's okay," Clara said as if she were talking to her doll. "Mommy's going to get a raise."

"What?" Dad said, turning to stare at Clara with that look of his.

"Sweetie, what do you mean?" Mom blurted out, her face splotchy with red, the way her skin turned when she's mad, scared, or embarrassed.

"You're gonna be pomoted," Clara told her, not quite using the right word.

I was keeping really quiet. I didn't want them to send me up to my room. It was almost time for my favorite program, and unlike Todd and everyone else I knew, we still only had two TVs — the big one downstairs in our living room and an old, tiny black and white TV in the garage where castoffs and Dad's vet stuff were stored.

Mom looked up at Dad and kind of chuckled. It was a strange laugh, though, like it wobbled or something. It wasn't like Mom disbelieved what Clara had said, but more like Mom wasn't sure what to do except laugh.

Mom turned her back on Clara and me. She looked up at Dad, and wiping her face on the apron, the one she wore whenever she cooked dinner, she said, "I wish that was true. There is a position coming up, but I'm not even up for consideration. I haven't been at the company long enough, Charlie."

Dad didn't say anything. He just picked up his calendar book and sighed. Then he walked over to the table my folks used as their desk and started shuffling papers around.

The next day, sure as seeds turn into plants, Mom told us that her boss had named her head of the department, passing over three guys who'd been working at the company for years. She didn't look all that happy about it, though, and she and Dad had another talk with Clara.

I didn't understand why that stuff bothered my parents so much. I thought it was cool that Clara could tell the future. I wished she'd do it more often so I could avoid the bad stuff that was going to happen, or at least be prepared for it.

Clara did tell me a week or so before Slurpinthal moved in that someone was coming. She pointed to the Simon's house when she said that, and then she stuck her thumb in her mouth. She never did that anymore, or at least she didn't used to, before Slurpinthal came.

After she told me about the new neighbor, Clara's nightmares started happening more frequently — in fact, almost every night. I always woke up when she screamed, but Mom and Dad never heard since they slept downstairs.

I wished, sometimes, that I could ignore Clara, but I couldn't stay in bed when I heard her in her room crying her eyes out. I had to get up and calm her down. Clara often didn't remember what she'd dreamed. She just stared at me when I asked, then sucked her thumb and held Babydoll with a grip tighter than Dad's vise.

On the morning when my parents decided we should all go over to the Simon's, I mean Slurpinthal's house, Clara was staring up at me with wide, frightened eyes. Her eyes looked like they did when she'd just had one of her nightmares. I put my arm around her and patted Babydoll. Then Clara smiled a little, but it was kind of a shaky smile. I knew exactly what she was feeling. I didn't mention that my stomach felt sick.

Mom had baked some cookies to take to Slurpinthal. Dad was carrying a baby rubber plant that he'd transferred into one of Mom's pots. Mom always said that making pots was the way she relaxed, so she made lots of pots. I liked to watch her on the potter's wheel. She wet and molded the clay, then cut off strips. It was like magic. The wheel went round and round, and the clay oozed up under her hands.

With just a touch of a finger or the edge of her palm, Mom formed all kinds of different shapes — tall, skinny ones that she called high fluted vases, fatter ones that were like old-fashioned milk bottles, pitchers for iced tea, roly-poly cookie jars with lids, skinny and fat mugs with comfortable handles on the sides, and platters. But more popular than any other pieces were the short, fat planter pots like the one Dad was taking to Mr. Slurpinthal.

Mom loved to decorate everything with her drippy colors. She used lots of cobalt blue and a special green that was the exact shade of leaves or grass. Some of her pots had clay leaves or snakelike trims that she wound around the pots like vines clinging to a wall. The pot Dad was taking to Mr. Slurpinthal had just been fired for the second time. That meant it had gone into the oven to bake twice. It was one of the plainer ones, only dribbled down the sides with cobalt blue.

Mom's kiln oven hid in a corner of our backyard, surrounded by a walkway of gravel all around it to keep any accidental fire from spreading. It had a cover over it that Dad had built, which sat up on top of a frame.

The kiln got super-hot, so Clara wasn't allowed to get close to it. I stayed away, too. I didn't want to accidentally bump it with my wheelchair. That would be a big no-no.

Sometimes Clara and I made pots at the long table at the other side of the backyard, but our pots never looked like Mom's. She was a professional, although she said she wasn't. Since her real work was handling the accounts at Crestlon Industries and now being head of the department, I guess she couldn't be a professional potter, although that's what she really liked to do.

Last week, Mom fired two of my pots. She put them in her pottery kiln and turned the heat up really high. The clay had to cook in the oven before it was ready for the painting glaze. Then, after you applied the paint, the pot cooked a second time in the kiln. I think the glaze was what made the pots so pretty. It was always a surprise because you could never tell what the finished product would look like until it had been fired the second time. Then the glaze turned shiny and the colors melded.

I kept my two finished pots in my room. The blue one I used for paperclips. The green one held my batteries. So far, Clara has never had anything fired. I think Mom was afraid that my sister's projects might blow up in the kiln. That's what happened when there were air bubbles in the clay.

If a pot had any air bubbles, it would destroy everything else being fired, so it was a big risk. Clara didn't seem to care. She said once the clay was fired, it couldn't be changed anymore. She preferred playing with the clay rather than making pots.

I was thinking about all that as we headed out the front door. Clara was clinging to my hand. I wished she wouldn't do that because she was using her death-grip. I knew I couldn't pry her hand off. I wouldn't have done that anyway. I figured if I could help her not be so afraid, then it would be worth having my hand squeezed into a pretzel.

Clara was wearing her coat, even though it wasn't cold outside. When I glanced down, she looked smaller somehow than usual, as if she'd shrunk. The collar of her jacket was standing up, and it was like she was hiding inside it. If she were a turtle, her head would be covered in jacket.

Dad and Mom had already walked out into the front yard. They looked back at us and whispered to each other.

"Clara, would you push me?" I asked. I didn't usually permit anyone to do that. I preferred to propel myself, but Clara's thumb was in her mouth, and her eyes were wild as the winds on an autumn day. I thought she needed to push. She needed to find something to take her mind off visiting the new neighbor.

Clara nodded. Her long ash brown hair bobbed back and forth. A strand made its way out of the back of her coat where she'd tucked it. She didn't notice. She was kissing her doll, telling it that everything was going to be okay.

Clara placed Babydoll on my lap, tenderly tucking the scraps of fabric around it and then the baby blanket that Mom had given her. It was obvious that Clara didn't want the doll's plastic skin to get cold. I didn't say anything. Clara believed that Babydoll was real.

Anyway, when I asked her to push, I figured I'd end up holding the silly thing, so I wasn't surprised. I was kind of resigned to it.

Hopefully, Tom Sumpers wouldn't be hanging out in my neighborhood on a Sunday.

Clara stood taller when I asked her to push me, but she wasn't very big yet, so to help her out, I gave the wheels a forward heave with my hands. Together we made it over the threshold and out through the door. We didn't bother locking a wheel as we headed down the slight incline of the ramp. I did brake a bit, not wanting Clara to fall. I didn't think she'd notice. Her head was up. Her hands were gripping the handles of my chair. She'd taken on the responsibility as if I depended on her.

When we reached the bottom of the driveway, she bent down and said, "Do you think he'll be mean?"

I turned my head and looked up at her, then shrugged. "If he is, we'll never talk to him again. Ok?"

Clara glanced over at Dad. He was frowning because we were being slow, but I saw that Mother had grabbed his arm and stopped him from interfering, so they were just standing there watching.

"Let's go," I told my sister, and she pushed with all her might. That time I didn't move the wheels. I let her be the one to move us forward. It wasn't that I was being cruel. I knew she was strong enough. I didn't worry about that. I worried about the fact that she wasn't seeing into the future. It appeared that she had no idea what was going to happen when we went to visit the new neighbor.

Chapter Three:

Meeting Slurpinthal

We arrived at the door as a family unit, my father in front, my mother knocking at the door, and Clara and me hanging back a bit. The door was brick red with a funny-looking wreath on it, not the kind people hang at Christmastime, but something that looked more like a witch's broom in miniature. The straw part at the bottom was tied with curly leaves, all dried out and brown. The top of it had small buttons glued on. I moved my chair forward to check it over. Clara grabbed at her doll and yanked it back into her arms just as the door slowly opened.

"A family?" someone hiding behind the door whined with a voice that sounded like the speaker was talking through a garden hose.

My father cleared his throat and started to speak. Mom beat him to it. "We're the Greens," she said. "We live next door."

I looked up at Clara and grimaced. I hated it when Mom said our name that way. It was bad enough when the kids at school questioned me as to whether I was lettuce leaves or spinach leaves. Real funny, right? Imagine going through school being called *The Salad*.

Usually, Clara giggled over that, but she wasn't smiling. She was staring at the door, wondering if Mr. Slurpinthal was going to show himself. Frankly, I hoped he wouldn't.

22

Dad was still clearing his throat. He coughed once more and said, "We've brought some cookies and a plant to welcome you to the neighborhood, Mr. Slurpinthal."

The door started to shiver and quake. I wheeled backward and collided with my sister.

"Ow!" she screamed, breaking into a curdling screech.

I suppose it does hurt when a wheelchair runs over your foot, but my sister was known for her excesses. Her wails when she got wounded were newsworthy. That moment was no exception.

Whether the new neighbor had decided to hide behind his door or not, the screams of my sister made the subject a done deal. Dad pushed forward, demanding, "Do you have a band-aid, my good man? She never stops howling until we apply one. You know how it is, right?"

The foot in the door, the people out in the street watching to see what was causing that horrific noise, and the fact that we'd brought gifts — one of those things, or all of them, weakened the man's hesitation. The door swung open, and we walked (and wheeled) ourselves inside.

Mr. Slurpinthal was short, shorter than I would have been if I could have stood up. I don't mean the man was a little person. One of the students at school was designated that way, although he preferred to be called a *person of short stature*. He was only a second grader, so I didn't know him well. Our teacher had explained the terminology. She said never to call them Midgets. That was the bad name.

But Mr. Slurpinthal didn't look like Stevie, the second grader, whose arms and legs were shorter than the rest of him. Mr. Slurpinthal looked strange, but not because of his height. His nose looked squatty. His mouth seemed crooked and wasn't exactly in the middle of his jaw like it should be, and his hair was an upturned broom in pumpkin orange.

23

Dad had planned to hand Mr. Slurpinthal the potted plant, but he took one look at Mr. Slurpinthal's arms, which were crossed, and darted a look about the room in hopes he'd see an appropriate spot to put it down. Mother wasn't bothered by that at all. She just thrust her cookies into the man's face.

"Welcome to Daffodil Lane," Mom told him, and then steered one of his hands into accepting the plate.

Strangely, Clara had stopped rampaging the moment we'd set foot in the man's house. Tears still swam in her eyes and across the sprinkling of freckles, which grew more abundant every summer. Her thumb was back in her mouth, and she was sucking harder than a baby starved for a meal.

Mr. Slurpinthal stared at the cookies in his hands. He acted like he didn't know what to do with them. I figured someone ought to tell him what they were for.

"You eat them," I said. "I mean you eat the cookies, not the plant."

Mr. Slurpinthal's eyes darted to the cookies. He tilted his head and then looked at me.

"You're the boy that . . ."

He didn't go on. He just stared at me, his little angled head rocking this way and that.

"The boy," he finished, then nodded his head.

My sister took out her thumb and started to scream again. I shook my finger at her.

"Don't you dare," I ordered.

Mr. Slurpinthal's eyes slid from side to side like one of the cat clocks I'd seen in a Mickey Mouse cartoon. The clock had a tail that kept time with its eyes. Mr. Slurpinthal didn't have a tail, but he began to sputter, going something like this: "bbbbbbbbbbbbbbbbb."

"Maybe we've come at a bad time," my mother said, grabbing my father's arm.

Dad's eyes were flitting from Mom to Mr. Slurpinthal and back. He gulped, cleared his throat, and began to speak. "Perhaps . . ."

"Bbbbut you mmmmmmmust sit dddddown," our new neighbor said. Then he turned and left, leaving us staring at each other and the closed door of what we figured must be the kitchen.

Clara sucked on her thumb so loudly, we all turned to look at her. Mom, with her hands free of the cookies, walked over to my sister and pulled her thumb free. "You must stop that, Clara. It is not just bad manners and unsanitary, but it's hard on your teeth."

My sister was considering whether to launch into another tirade of temper or to stubbornly return to her thumb sucking when Mr. Slurpinthal returned.

He had left the cookies in the other room. He strode over to my father, took the plant from him, and smelled the leaves.

"What is this?" he asked.

My father broke into a smile of contentment. Dad loved to talk about his plants.

I looked around for the chairs that everyone was supposed to sit in. Of course, I'd brought my own — small joke, there. But for the others in the family, there were no chairs, no couches, no stools, not even wooden boxes for plopping your bottom on.

I figured with Dad talking about plants, this visit was going to be much, much longer than planned, and with no place to sit, it would be very uncomfortable for Mom and Clara.

25

Dad was again going through his throat clearing and his nervous twitches where he jerked at his collar, unbuttoned his shirt's top button, and then rebuttoned it again. He had just opened his mouth to begin a long speech about the wonder of the baby rubber plant, this one a variegated yellow, when Mr. Slurpinthal took a bite out of one of the plant's leaves.

Dad's speech dried up. "No," was all he could get out as Mr. Slurpinthal swallowed and munched on another leaf.

Mom, without waiting for an invitation, plopped down on the bare floor — did I mention that the house, at least the part we were in, didn't have carpeting or even throw rugs?

Clara, observing Mom, decided she wanted to sit, too.

"I need a chair," she told Mr. Slurpinthal. "Don't you have any chairs?"

Mr. Slurpinthal stopped chewing. He was on his third leaf, but he paused before reaching for the fourth.

"Share?" He picked a leaf and held it out to my sister.

Dad's mouth was open. He looked like a hooked fish still pumping its gills in hopes of getting one last breath of air.

Mom was fanning herself. Her face had paled and then turned red. She kept wetting her lips, like she was afraid they were so dry they were in danger of cementing together.

Clara switched thumbs. I wondered if she saved her left one for emergencies.

"So, you like plants? Good thing this one isn't poisonous. Do they have plants where you're from?" I asked our brand-new neighbor.

"Share?" he asked cautiously, not extending a leaf to me as he'd done for my sister.

The plant was down to its last four leaves. It was clear that Mr. Slurpinthal wasn't enthusiastic about giving me one.

I shook my head and said, "No, thank you," to be polite. "Where are you from?" I asked again, thinking that maybe he hadn't heard my question.

"There and not there," he said, placing the plant down on the floor beside him. "You go now?"

Clara was nodding her head up and down. Her hood had fallen, and her long hair wiggled like snakes.

Mr. Slurpinthal took a step back, eyeing the hair as if he thought it might hiss at him.

"Yes, it is time," my mother agreed, rising slowly. She was still fanning herself with her hand, but her face didn't look red anymore. The expression on it reminded me of the way she'd looked the time she'd come down with the flu — just before she fainted.

"Uh, Dad?" I said, but it was too late. Mom did a quick snowman melt and landed in a puddle of limbs, right in the middle of the floor.

"Meggie,' Dad called out and rushed over to her, but Mr. Slurpinthal was not only closer but faster.

He bent over my mother, touched the top of her nose, and said, "Baaaaaaaaap."

Mom opened her eyes. The first thing she saw was the neighbor peering down at her. She let out a scream almost equal to Clara's.

"Meggie," Dad repeated, sliding into a position that managed to wedge Mr. Slurpinthal to the side.

I wheeled myself into action.

"You better move back, Mr. Slurpinthal. Whenever Mom faints, she vomits right after."

"I move here," he told me, wrinkling up his nose as if he'd just smelled something bad.

"Mommy, let's go," Clara said, edging close enough to grab at my wheelchair.

It was just as well that she pulled me back a couple of feet. As I'd said, Mom always erupts after a faint.

Dad and Mr. Slurpinthal both got sprayed. So did the floor and the plant Mr. Slurpinthal liked so much.

"Oh, I'm so sorry," Mom cried out. Then she spilled out even more in a stinky puddle about an inch away from Mr. Slurpinthal's purple shoes.

Dad helped Mom up. She was looking a little less green by then. When Dad handed Mom a hankie, and she wiped her mouth and face, she began to look more like her normal self.

Unfortunately, Mr. Slurpinthal's spine drooped sideways, and he paled once he saw what had happened to his new plant.

"BBBBBBBBBBBBBBB," he cried.

Dad patted him on the back. "I'll bring you another one. Don't worry. I have lots of them."

I'm not sure our neighbor understood all that, but it did stop his string of B's. He turned about three times, clapped his hands, and said, "You wwwwwwill go now?"

"I'll be glad to clean up the mess," Dad said, but Mr. Slurpinthal was already directing us toward the door.

"Go now?" he repeated just in case we hadn't gotten the right idea.

It took only seconds for us to be standing outside. We heard the wooden door slam. The lock bolted an instant later.

"Well, that was an adventure," my father said as he took Mom's hand.

"I'm so embarrassed. I can't believe I did that. I'll never be able to look him in the eyes again," Mom sighed. "What must he think of us?"

Clara and I glanced at each other.

"Babydoll says he's an alien."

I started laughing, but Mom and Dad frowned. "Why do you say that? What makes you think he's . . ."

A strange look passed between them. I wasn't sure what it meant, but I'd seen it before. The conversation was over.

I grinned and tried to cover it. I shouldn't have pretended to yawn. Mom sprinted over to lay her hand on my forehead.

"Are you sick?" she asked. "Are you having a bad reaction?"

I sighed.

That night, just before I went to bed, I stared out my window at the house next door. The bedroom was lit up like the grand opening of a new department store. I wondered what the alien was doing. Was he reporting on our strange visit? Was he telling his people all about the funny Earthlings who lived next door? Or was he developing secret plans to pay us back for the way we'd welcomed him to the cul-de-sac?

Chapter Four:

Forbidden to Speak About It

The next day at breakfast, Dad sat down to eat with us. That was rather unusual. He usually left early to start his rounds. Horse people and farmers always got up with the sun, or so Dad always said.

Dad had made us pancakes, which he never does on a school day. Clara and I exchanged glances, wondering what was up. We didn't have to ponder long.

Dad poured himself a full cup of coffee, sat down in the chair next to Mom, shoved his elbows on the table, and stared at the coffee swirling around. He'd just stirred in a whole spoonful of sugar, but I don't think that was why he was staring at the coffee.

"There's something we need to discuss," Dad said, once the ripples on his coffee calmed down a bit. He looked up at Mom and gestured like he was trying to get her to handle it. She shook her head, picked up her cup of tea and blinked. I think it was a sign, but of what I wasn't sure.

The clock was making growling sounds. It was old, and I think it was hoping that it could scratch itself out as it aired its final seconds of clock-ticking death. Each time it got to the ten, it stuck and pounced back and forth a bit, before it crawled on up to the eleven. Then it sighed and traveled on.

I was thinking about the groaning of the clock and whether it knew its time had almost cuckooed out, when Dad said, "You children have to be nicer to Mr. Slurpinthal. Your mother and I don't want you calling him an alien anymore."

Mom started tapping her foot, a nervous habit she had when she was sitting down. I wondered why it was always the right foot that tapped and not the left. Did that have any relationship with the way Clara usually sucked her left thumb and not her right?

Dad took a moment to take a swallow of coffee. He looked at my sister and then at me. "You have to be the leader, Kyle. You have to guide Clara into knowing what's right and what's wrong. She looks up to you, you know."

Clara was wiggling in her chair. I thought she was embarrassed by my father's words and trying to slip down off the chair and escape, but she was only reaching over to pick up Babydoll. As if Dad weren't lecturing, she calmly began to feed her doll, using the spoon to deliver bits of pancake to the doll's plastic mouth.

Dad cleared his throat. He didn't usually do that as much when he had a mug of coffee in his hands. Apparently, the throat irritation didn't stop him from lecturing. His brow darkened, and two busy eyebrows grew thicker and lower. His eyes narrowed into concentration. He wasn't using his x-ray vision to stare into us at that moment, but he looked like he was using his power of mind to remove the word "alien" from our heads.

I stuffed another heavily loaded forkful of pancake into my mouth. It was dripping with honey and butter. Naturally, a couple of drops of sticky hit the right pocket of my shirt.

I rolled over to the sink to rub out the spot. I was wearing my favorite t-shirt — a faded black one with white lettering.

The water spot left a bigger smudge on my shirt, and my *Be yourself, everyone else is already taken. — Oscar Wilde shirt* still smelled of butter and honey. Was that a good thing or a bad one? Would anyone notice the stain or the smell? Should I change?

"Just leave it," Mom said. "I'll wash it tonight. I have to do a load of blouses, anyway."

Whether I had to change or not, I still had more pancakes on my plate. I slid back into my place at the table and dug in.

"Did you hear me, Kyle?"

Dad's left eye had begun to twitch. He was taking this lecture thing seriously. I chewed another mouthful and thought about it.

I guess I should have had more common sense than to argue with anything in Dad's speech, but the whole sermon thing at 7:00 in the morning was really getting to me. I put down my fork, glanced down at the quarter-size spot on my shirt, and said, "Why shouldn't we say that, Dad? You saw him yourself. Do you think he's normal?"

"Kyle!" my mother cried out so forcefully that Clara dropped her spoon. Tiny bits of pancake scattered all over her shirt and pants. I guess I wasn't the only one who'd have to do a quick change after breakfast.

Mother stood up, as much to assist Clara in cleaning up the mess as to glare at me for saying what I'd said. I blinked and looked back, completely puzzled. I mean, I hadn't called Mr. Slurpinthal a bad word or anything. Why were Mom and Dad so huffy about it?

"I told you that you are not to call our new neighbor an alien. You don't know how long he's been in the country. He might not have been born here. Maybe his parents didn't speak English. Maybe he never learned English in school. You have no right to be snooty just because someone has difficulty with the language," Mom said, wiping away a tear.

Dad was nodding and trying to drink coffee at the same time. He spilled some on his pants and grimaced. It looked like the whole Green family would be washing clothes that evening.

"What's wrong with saying he's an alien?" I asked, reaching down for my fork.

"I think you've had enough to eat," Mom stated, grabbing away my plate.

I opened my mouth and started to argue, but both Mom and Dad were looking at me like I'd just said the "sh" word at the table.

I clamped my mouth shut and started to push my wheelchair back so I could head up to my room for a fresh change of shirts. I figured that the gray one with *Though no one can go back and make a brand-new beginning, anyone can start from now and make a brand-new ending — Carl Bard* would still be clean enough to wear. I'd only had it on for a couple of hours on Sunday — just long enough to visit the alien I wasn't supposed to call an alien.

As I headed for the elevator, my hand froze as I heard my sister say, "But Mr. Slurpinthal is an alien. I can see it."

Clara had just broken two rules — one: talking back, and two: talking about that thing she wasn't supposed to be able to do.

I wheeled myself around the corner so I was hidden but could still peek back at the table. I wanted to see what my parents were going to do about Clara's statement.

Dad stood up, downed the rest of his coffee, and headed for the door. "Sorry, Meggie. I'm late for the pig farmer down on Stormy Lane. He's got a stallion that's ready to . . ." His eyes glanced in the direction I'd gone and then back to Clara. Without completing his thought, he gave Mom a traveling kiss, and shot out the door faster than she could get a word out.

33

"Dr. Samuel Green," Mom called out, but it was too late. The front door was already slamming shut.

Mom picked up the handful of dirty plates and marched over to the sink. Clara giggled. I gave her a look from around the corner that I hoped resembled one of Dad's and wheeled myself over to the platform at the foot of the stairs.

Riding the lift up, I thought about how Clara always got away with things that I never could. Then I remembered not only what she'd said, but how she'd said it — no finger in the mouth, no watery, fearful eyes. Was Clara already accepting the fact that the newest member of Daffodil Lane was someone who'd come from another planet?

As I slid off my t-shirt and replaced it with the gray one, I debated asking her if she'd dreamed last night. She often didn't remember anything, but what if she'd dreamed about the man's spaceship? What if she'd dreamed something really important? Could I get her aside before Mom scooped us up and rushed us over to our respective schools?

I started to run a comb through my hair before remembering that just the week before I'd had the hairstylist buzz it. No more curls for me. It was bad enough that I sometimes had a doll in my backpack. I certainly didn't need *curls* to make me the brunt of more jokes.

I threw a look at the mirror, nodded at what I saw, and rolled on down the carpeted hallway, heading for Clara's room. I knocked and then entered.

"Clara, this is important," I said. "Have you had another dream about our neighbor?"

She'd been wrapping her doll in a pillowcase. She peeled the fabric back so the ugly thing looked like a papoose. I wondered if her pre-school class had been studying Native Americans, but I didn't ask.

I wanted her to stick to the important thing. Did she know something she hadn't told me?

"Yes, he came into my bedroom."

I shut the door so Mom wouldn't hear if she happened to be passing by on the way to her built-in office in the hall closet.

I turned to examine my sister. "For real?"

She laughed and shook her head. "I saw him come, but he didn't yet."

Whatever explanation my sister was about to offer, it was interrupted by my mother opening the door. "You two ready to leave?" she asked.

Clara nodded and set her doll down on the bed. Because she wasn't allowed to bring Babydoll to pre-school, she bent down and kissed her.

"Mommy will be right back," she whispered to Babydoll. The doll continued to stare at the ceiling.

Clara's shirt was still spotted with pancake droppings. Mom's eyes flew to the stains. She let out a deep sigh, then shook her head. Glancing down at her watch, she tapped it and said, "No time to change. Let's go, kids."

"But the alien," Clara said, looking toward the window. I glanced out, but my sister's bedroom didn't have the wonderful view like mine did. Hers looked down on the backyard. You could see the tree where the bird's nest had fallen, the small swing set that Mom and Dad had assembled for us, and the plastic wading pool that was lying upside down on the grass. Mom made us dump it out every day, fearing mosquitoes would hatch if we left any water in it. There were definitely no aliens in the backyard — at least none I could see.

When I turned my chair about to follow Mom, I saw her face turning red. That was what happened whenever she got mad at one of us. I was glad it wasn't me who'd just called our new neighbor an alien. Mom might not have time to deal with such things as we rushed through the hall and down the stairs (me on the elevator, which actually takes longer than walking down) and out the front door, but mothers always seem to have a long memory. It was a sure bet we'd both be lectured at dinner.

As we headed out the door, I caught sight of a cool-looking jet scribbling messages in the sky. "Whoa, look at that!" I yelled.

In spite of the fact that Mom was already grabbing the door of the car and shoving Clara into the backseat, I stopped to watch, staring up into the pale blueness of a cloudless sky. The pilot was really blasting along. I wondered if I'd hear the boom that jets made sometimes when they broke the sound barrier. "Do it!" I whispered.

"Kyle!" Mom yelled.

I pressed my hands against the chair's wheels and resumed my pushing. "Coming," I told her.

Just as the lift at the back of our van was hauling both my chair and me up, the boom happened. The jet sped through a ripple, and the air thundered in reply.

"Cool," I roared. Of course, my eyes were still watching where the jet had creased the sky. But the skywriter was gone.

"You know what, Mom," I said, "If the Marines would take someone like me, I'd be first in line to join up."

"I know you would, Kyle," Mom said as she raised her arm over the back of the car seat and neatly backed up into the street.

"Wait! It's the alien," my sister cried out.

Mr. Slurpinthal was waving his arms like a windmill, trying to get our attention. Mom drove forward again a couple of yards and pushed the window button into the down position so she could talk to him.

"Good morning, Mr. Slurpinthal," Mom said. "How are you today?"

Mom's face was all lit up, like she liked the guy. I watched her intently. What was going on? Had the alien done something to make my mother gush each time she saw him?

"What crashes this noise?" the guy asked, clutching at his ears.

I stared up at the sky, hoping the pilot would fly back around. Besides, I was afraid that if I looked at the alien, I'd either break into laughter or blurt out a question that would make my mom's face go all red again.

"It was a plane, an airplane," Mom told him. "The National Guard flies out of Moffett Field on training flights."

Mom's knee started to twitch. She glanced at the clock on the dashboard. Her fingers played the piano on the steering wheel.

"Is regular? No thing special?"

Mom's eyes swung back. "Don't worry, Mr. Slurpinthal. They don't do that often. They're not supposed to do it at all. All the neighbors will complain. But there are always some new guys flying. They're so young, you know."

Mr. Slurpinthal's face chewed on that a moment. First his eyebrows moved in and out. Then his cheeks puffed and unpuffed. Next, his lips opened and closed. I wondered if his ears would join in. Sure enough. They were next. Up and down. Up and down.

"Mom didn't see that, of course. She was checking her watch.

"I'm sorry, Mr. Slurpinthal. We've got to go. We're late," she explained.

"Go? Ah. I see. Go. Yes," Mr. Slurpinthal said, coming closer to stare in the car's window as if he were unsure what he'd see inside.

"Children present. Where is father-dad? He go?" he asked.

Mother let out a whistle of irritation.

"Really, Mr. Slurpinthal. I must leave. We are really, really late."

"Good. Late is good. It is early that makes for rudeness, yes?"

Mother raced the engine, put the car in reverse again, and slowly began to back out into the street. I guess Mr. Slurpinthal knew enough about cars to move his feet out of the way. When I looked back, he was still standing there, his eyes slightly crossed, his hands folded, but still moving up and down in a rolling kind of way — like his arms were the ocean and he was trying to show us the swell of surf.

I didn't mean to, but my hand flung itself up and waved. He must have seen it because his lips parted, and his teeth grinned at me. I stared at him as Mom drove down the street. Mr. Slurpinthal's eyes held mine until we turned on Robinson to head for my school.

Todd was waiting for me out on the steps of the building.

"Hey, what took you so long?" he called out, causing at least ten kids to turn around and look. Todd wasn't paying attention. His eyes were on me, so of course, the other kids all turned to see my lift dropping down. I bet my face was as red as Mom's by the time I'd been lowered enough to push myself off the ramp.

By then, Todd had come closer. He knew not to grab my backpack or anything, like I needed help, which I didn't. I'd have kicked him if he tried it. But Todd did pat my shoulder and walk along beside me.

"Hey, how come you're so late?" he asked again before I could get a word out.

He was gnawing on a bagel, the kind with strawberry cream cheese. I'd just had a breakfast of pancakes, but my mouth watered at the sight of his snack. Todd broke off a piece — a ridiculously small piece — handed it to me, and went on chewing.

My mother called out goodbye, and I waved. Clara didn't notice. I could tell she was thinking about something, lost in her own world. I doubt she even knew I'd left the van. I smiled, shoved the piece of bagel in my mouth and let the sweetness coat my tongue.

Meanwhile, Todd was chattering about some math test he was having that day. He'd had trouble with his homework and wanted to know if I could help him.

"Sure," I sneered. "Like I should tutor you?"

Todd was a math genius. I couldn't imagine him wanting my help. I could barely solve a simple equation, but he was already juggling two variables in something he called two-step equations. I'd thought that was the dance my mom and dad were learning.

Fortunately, the bell rang, saving me from further confessions of ignorance. We both went our way, Todd taking the steps two by two, me doing double-time to get up the rather steep ramp that took me into the main building.

"Can I help?"

Elizabeth, the girl with whale blubber around her middle and the ugliest nose in the whole school, had sneaked up behind me. Without waiting for me to turn her down, she plastered her fat hands on my wheelchair and pushed me the rest of the way up the ramp.

"Thanks," I managed to say as she sped off to class.

"Anytime," she yelled back, giving me a smile that showed the metal braces she wore under her lips.

For the hundredth time, I wondered what that would feel like. It sure couldn't be anything pleasant. The other kids tormented Elizabeth even more than they did me. Even the nice kids acted mean to ugly, fat girls.

"I can't believe you let her do that," Bobby from social studies said, giving my wheelchair a spin on one wheel. "She's a pariah, you know."

I had no idea what a pariah was, but I nodded, then waved as he threw his backpack over his shoulder and went galloping off to class. I saw him get tagged for it. Some preppie issued him a "get out of school late pass." I chuckled and wheeled myself back to the first classroom. I just made it in before the second bell rang.

"Ooh, I saw Elizabeth Jornick helping you up the ramp," said Claude Kittler.

"Jerk," I muttered under my breath just before slipping into my spot on the third row at the rear.

"I heard that," Claude said, smirking as if he'd scored the winning goal.

The teacher had begun roll call. She gave both of us a teacher glare. We mutually declared a truce with a shrug and a nod.

Meanwhile, I pulled out my English essay and made sure it had my name on it. Mrs. Hatter collected them right off. I noticed Claude didn't have one.

The day continued, not worse than most and no better. At least I didn't run into Tom Sumpers after school. Dad picked me up and took me with him for his last veterinary appointment.

Bluegrass Farm is famous throughout the county for its Arabian pintos. Now, just in case you're not a horse enthusiast, I'd better explain about that. Yes, I know that a purebred Arabian can only be bay, chestnut, roan, gray, or black. If you don't know what all those colors are, it doesn't really matter. Let's just say that the first three colors are mainly shades of brown. But at Bluegrass Farm, they have bred their purebreds to mares of color. The result is an Arab that isn't purebred any longer but has large patches of black and white. Bluegrass Farm has the most beautiful horses in the world. At least, that's what my father says, and he's a top vet.

The only problem is that when Bluegrass Farm was breeding for bright color, they sort of neglected the intelligence part of the equation. Dad says there isn't a single horse on the farm with more common sense than a thimble.

But that is good for Dad's wallet. The farm keeps him coming almost weekly to patch up legs, slather medicine on skinned noses and withers, or to free one of the horses from their latest piece of mischief.

That was the case on that Monday. Painted Starfish, named because of the design on her rear flank, had entangled herself in a piece of fencing. By the time we arrived, she'd been freed from the fence, but she was standing with her head down, her shoulders wet with sweat, and her body shaking like a mound of jelly.

I'm not a huge fan of horses, mainly because they're even bigger than Tom Sumter. They bite, too. In fact, the very last time I tried to help Dad out, one of them peeled back his five-inch-thick lips, smiled at me with slimy green teeth the size of meat grinders, and sampled a taste of my flesh.

When I'd finished screaming like a rabid wolf, Dad treated me with some of his animal medicine. The goop took my pain away, but the next day it looked like someone had painted me in deep reds and purples. And it hurt for weeks.

Dad told me later he'd been bitten before. He said it was part of being a vet.

I turned my wheelchair around when he said that, so I could stare up at Dad's face.

"So why would you want to be a horse vet if the mean things are always trying to bite you?"

For some reason that cracked Dad up. He almost spilled the medicine he was trying to get down a horse's big ugly mouth.

"Son," he said, shaking his head, "I really wonder about that sometimes. Especially every time my insurance payment comes due."

Mom told me that Dad loves being a vet, but I can't tell you why. He was always getting gunk — usually the bright orange kind — spilt all over his shirt. He often stank of urine and cow poop, and he'd had his foot trampled on at least nine times that I know about. Once he even had to limp around all the farms with a cast on his foot, which he needed to wear for months.

Mom kept threatening to make him sleep in the garage because the cast smelled like farm animals. I don't know why she complained so much. Dad always smelled like horses, cows, and stinky medicine. But, anyway, Dad finally got the cast off, and Mom stopped grumbling.

Mom and Dad still held hands and kissed when they thought Clara and I weren't around. As Todd said, with a disgusted look on his face, my parents acted like a couple of love-sick teenagers.

Todd's parents were the opposite. They were always arguing about everything. They had big cat fights. At least that's what Todd told me. He also said that sometimes his mother threw things at his father. Last summer his parents even split up for a couple of months.

His father moved into a hotel, and his mom supposedly cried all the time. Then at the end of the summer, Todd's father moved back in.

I couldn't imagine Mom throwing things at Dad. And neither of my parents would ever yell. I guessed I was pretty lucky.

Chapter Five:

Prejudice and Disbelief

Todd didn't like to talk about his parents. I couldn't blame him. I knew that his parents were all kissy for a while, but then they started yelling again. Todd got scared. He wasn't doing his homework, and he never wanted to go home. He asked my mom if he could stay with us for a week. My parents were cool about it. They treated Todd like he was one of the family. He even had to do chores and show them his homework every night.

But then his mother called and said he had to come back. After that, Todd wasn't supposed to tell me how things were going at home. I hoped his parents didn't get a divorce. That's what Todd was big-time worried about.

Whoops. I just did it again. I was telling you about Painted Starfish, a filly, which is a young girl horse, and then, I went off and talked about Todd's parents. I don't know how that happened. I didn't mean it to. It reminds me of cats, how you can tell them to stay in a place, and they just ignore you and mosey off whenever they feel like it. That's what my thoughts do.

But back to the Arabians at Bluegrass Farm. I didn't mind when Dad asked me to pet Painted Starfish. She wasn't a big horse. She was what Dad called a yearling. That meant when she hurt herself, she was only a baby. Just imagine running around and getting caught in a wire fence when you were only a year old. Horses were pretty amazing that way.

Once I watched a mare giving birth. The foal's feet came out first. I thought that was weird. But maybe that's why a newborn foal can stand up right away. I mean, if the feet were the first things born . . . Dad would probably laugh if I said that. He thinks I should read up on horses and cows, but I'm never going to be a vet.

I'm going to be an astronaut — at least if I ever get to walk again. If not, I guess I'll be a lawyer. You can be a lawyer and still be stuck in a wheelchair. I saw it on TV once. Besides, a lawyer can talk his way out of anything. That would be a good skill to have.

While I was holding Painted Starfish, the owner came out to see how we were doing. Dad told Mr. Carter that I was helping, but the man's face got all puckered up. He was chewing tobacco and spat some of it off to the side. I tried not to watch. I knew that baseball players chewed tobacco, but I wished they wouldn't. Dad said the stuff gives people cancer. I wouldn't want to have something in my mouth that could give me cancer.

Mr. Carter was eyeing me funny, like he thought I shouldn't be there, but I hadn't done anything wrong. I mean, I'd never be mean to a horse or anything, and I never yelled or made a lot of noise. I think it was pretty obvious, too, that I wasn't going to jump up and down and make the horses nervous, so I didn't know why Mr. Carter's eyes were glaring at me.

The owner spat into the bushes again and then turned to face my father.

"I don't think it's a real good idea to have your boy down here in the field," Mr. Carter said. "That wheelchair could tip over, and your boy might get hurt."

I knew from the way Mr. Carter's eyes were peeking at me from little slits in the sides, that he was really saying that a farm was no place for a boy in a wheelchair. Lots of people think that. They think

I shouldn't be at school or at the library or even at the grocery store. I don't know why. Being paralyzed isn't contagious, you know.

Oftentimes, I wished I hadn't gone to the church bazaar that day. It was a Saturday, a pretty day with sunbeams streaming down through the tree leaves. There was a breeze, not a big one, just the cooling-off, friendly kind. It's what made me think of the sunbeams. They were streaks across the air, shimmery, flying streaks. I remember blinking, wondering if everyone saw them, or it was just me on that particular day.

Of course, I knew everyone could see sunbeams. It wasn't like I was special or anything. It's just that a lot of people let things like that go past them, and they didn't *see* them. I heard music when it was playing, and others didn't. I mean, they could hear it when I pointed it out. But they didn't hear it until I said something. They just didn't notice.

Sunbeams were like that, and on that day, they glowed brightly. I thought that was a sign it was going to be a good day. I guess there's no such thing as a sign.

Dad had paused to listen to Mr. Carter, but when he said that about it's not being a good thing for me to be out in the field, Dad just turned away and started working on the filly, almost like he was ignoring the ranch owner. My father picked up a can of white gunk and painted it all over the wounds on Painted Starfish's front legs. The yearling quivered a bit, but she wasn't scared anymore. I think the salve tickled her more than hurt.

Then Dad gave the filly a Tetanus shot just to make sure she didn't get sick from her struggle with the wire. Meanwhile, Mr. Carter tried not to look at me but stared every time he thought I wasn't looking.

After Dad finishing doing what he needed to do for Painted Starfish, Dad gathered up the used syringe, the small bottle of medication Dad called a vial, and all of his trash. Carefully, taking care not to prick himself with the needle, he put them back into the leather vet bag that I was holding. I clutched it tight as Dad took a firm grip on the handgrips and started to push me. Unfortunately, one wheel of my chair had become stuck in the mud. Dad had to tug at it to break it free.

Stuff like that would have been a problem for some people, but Dad was strong. He half lifted the wheel while he was pushing me forward and then wheeled me back onto the path. Mr. Carter just watched, not even offering to help. He didn't say anything, either, but I could feel his eyes on my back. I'm sure he was thinking I was too much trouble, or that it wasn't safe for me to be out in his field, or maybe that he just didn't want me on his property at all.

I wished there were something I could say to convince him otherwise. I did help Dad as much as I could. I looked up things in his vet book when he asked me to. I got out the cotton balls and alcohol for cleaning injection sites. Sometimes I even counted out the pills and readied the bandages. I mean, I wasn't totally useless. At least I hoped I wasn't.

Mr. Carter dropped back to walk beside Dad. That was okay with me. I listened to the farmer's heavy crunch in the gravel of the path. Dad walked like a Native American, or the way it said in my history book that braves walked, so they wouldn't alert animals to their presence.

Dad's tread was light, but Mr. Carter would never be able to sneak up on a wild animal and watch him sleeping. Mr. Carter would take one step, and the rabbit or squirrel would jump up and speed away because the man was an extremely noisy walker.

As Dad moved me forward, we passed a field with yearling colts and fillies. They were all bucking, rearing, and staging pretend fights. Their satiny coats sparkled in the sun — black and white coats with high held tails and the small shapely heads of the Arabian horse. Mr. Carter had beautiful animals. Frisky ones, too, I decided, as I watched a colt come galloping up to the fence. It stopped no more than an inch away and stood there pawing at the ground, rolling its neck as if its neck were made of rubber.

I laughed softly. The colt, hearing my voice, eyed me with eyes white with fear. Apparently, it wasn't used to wheelchairs. It snorted loudly, pawed the ground, and then whirled away, leaving a cloud of dust.

My dad and Mr. Carter had stopped to watch. Dad made a comment I didn't hear. Mr. Carter coughed from all the dust, then got out his kerchief and blew. Dad pushed me forward, and we continued down the path toward the barn.

A small hawk was gliding in circles in the sky. He was probably a good fifteen feet up, not even aware of us. And yet, I knew hawks saw everything. Maybe he was staring down at us, wondering what we were doing, hoping we'd frighten a hare into running for cover.

As I stared upward, he seemed to drift lower. I could see his wingspan, the feathers streaked with white and hues of soft brown and dark. He called out, a lonely sound, a cry that lifted at the end like he was asking something.

I wished I could join him. I'd have wings even longer than his. I'd fly higher, flapping upward into the clouds. I closed my eyes and pictured it. The small hawk and I would battle the currents, riding them like a surfer on his wave. The air would be damp and cold because of the water vapor inside the small wisps of cloud.

We'd dance on the air drifts, bobbing in, out, and around the cloud. Hide and seek in the skies. Or maybe we'd race, stretching out our feather-covered muscles, powering each breath of wind with the beat of our flapping wings. We'd glance down and see a cougar or a deer.

We'd drop lower just to watch. Maybe, at the sight of us, a hare would bolt. Then we'd plunge like a . . .

"Kyle," Dad interrupted. "Did you hear Mr. Carter?"

The wheelchair had stopped. I hadn't even noticed. I glanced up. The hawk had gone. The sky was empty.

"What?" I asked.

Dad sighed. I knew that sound. He was impatient with me but trying not to show it.

"Mr. Carter asked if you were tired."

I shook my head.

"No, Sir. I was just thinking about hawks, wondering what it would be like to fly."

"Oh," he said, and we pushed on.

Mr. Carter wanted Dad to take a quick look at his favorite mare, Bay Meadows. She was in foal again, meaning that in a couple of months another frisky colt or filly would be dancing about at her side. I liked Bay Meadows. She was a quiet horse, quite different from her breed. She took carrots from my hands with a gentle tug. She nuzzled oats from my cupped palm and never tried to bite me. She and I were good friends.

As we entered the big barn where Mr. Carter stabled his prime breeders, he gave Dad a quick look.

"Couldn't your lad stay outside? I don't want him upsetting Bay Meadows."

Dad laughed, not cruelly. Dad was never cruel, not to anyone. His laugh was just a brief uplift of his lips accompanied by a quiet chuckle.

"Bay Meadows likes my son, Mr. Carter. Kyle seems to calm the mare. Watch and see."

I'd been hoping we'd visit Bay Meadows. As I said, she was one of the horses I liked. I dug in my sweatshirt jacket and pulled out the carrot I'd brought for her. I fingered it as I watched Mr. Carter's face.

People never realized how much could be read by the lines around the eyes or by the way eyebrows curled up or down. People didn't realize they had tiny wiggles at the corner of their mouths when they were stressed. All that gave them away and made them seem as readable as the pages of a book. I studied Mr. Carter's face, not because I didn't know what he was thinking, but because I wanted to see his face change when he saw the way Bay Meadows reacted to my presence.

Sure as butterflies have wings, the mare heard us coming, glanced up, and nickered. I doubted she was calling Mr. Carter. He was a businessman, not interested in whether his horses liked him or not. He didn't have a *horseman's empathy*, I'd heard my Dad say once.

Of course Dad hadn't known I was listening then. Comments heard when people don't know you're listening are the best. They're the meat of the sandwich, I think — the truth undisguised by careful wording.

Anyway, as Dad pushed me forward, Bay Meadows walked closer to her stall door. Her head dropped down. She began, I guess you'd call it nickering, but it was more like a rough-hewed purr, if you asked me. It showed she was excited to see me and clearly remembered that I was the boy who always brought her a carrot.

When Dad wheeled me close enough, I reached up and petted Bay Meadow under her muzzle. She liked that — the only horse, Dad had said, he'd ever seen that liked to be stroked there. Bay Meadow ignored everyone else and pressed into my hand. I scratched, while she murmured her purr-like rumbles of contentment.

"Well, I'll be," Mr. Carter said, "That horse does like your boy. I've never seen her take to anyone like that before."

I'd promised myself I'd watch the man's face just to see how it changed, but my eyes were concentrating, instead, on Bay Meadows. One had to pay attention to horses. Their ears told you everything. Bay Meadow's were forward in contentment, but she must be smelling the carrot. In a moment, those ears could swing back, and she might decide I was teasing her. Horses don't mind letting you know when they get impatient.

It was a good thing I was watching the mare and not Mr. Carter. Just at that moment, Bay Meadows raised her head to stare into my eyes. Her ears flicked back and forth, letting me know it was time to make the correct move. I did. I raised up the carrot and watched as her alfalfa green teeth bit into it.

Chewing her mouthful, she once more lowered her head for me to caress her. She didn't want me to scratch, I saw, just to pet her nose. I started to do so, but she shook her head, spraying me with small carrot fragments.

Dad laughed. Then Mr. Carter did too. I just wiped my face and offered the mare another bite of carrot. She bit off another piece just as my father opened the stall's lower door and darted in. Of course, the mare backed to allow him entry. Then, ignoring him, she resumed her position and took another bite of carrot.

Meanwhile, Mr. Carter watched as my Dad ran his hand over the mare's stomach. Dad had taken out the stethoscope from the bag sitting on my lap. He used that to listen for the foal's heartbeat.

"Sounds good," Dad said after a moment.

I was just placing the last piece of the carrot on my palm. Bay Meadow was such a lady, she watched and waited for me to balance it correctly. She knew she had a final bite coming, and unlike some of the other horses on the ranch, she wasn't pushy.

"Careful now, boy," Mr. Carter called out.

He didn't need to worry. I held my hand straight, my fingers down and out of the way. I'd been feeding carrots to horses for five or six years. I knew how to do it without losing a finger to an overeager horse.

The carrot finished, or at least being chewed, Bay Meadow, nuzzled my hand for a minute, probably checking to see if I had another. I didn't. Mom allowed only one per visit. She said we didn't have enough money to go around feeding other people's animals.

If Dad didn't always plead my case, Mom probably wouldn't have let me have even one. Since the accident, Mom has been worrying a lot about money. Dad, too, but at least he made sure I got a carrot.

I scratched Bay Meadow's muzzle for another minute and then told her goodbye. Mr. Carter gave me half a smile as Dad turned the wheelchair around. I wondered if that meant that the owner had forgotten his former prejudice, or was he just glad to see me going?

On the way home, Dad and I talked — or rather I talked. First, we discussed Mr. Carter a bit, Dad making sure my feelings hadn't gotten hurt. Of course they had been a little, but I didn't tell Dad that. No sense giving him pain. It wasn't his fault.

But after we cleared that up about Mr. Carter, I told Dad about what I'd seen the night Mr. Slurpinthal moved in. As I let out the whole story, Dad didn't interrupt or argue or anything. He just listened, so I got even more specific. I told him about the bright light that had turned my face and arms beet red with sunburn. I gave him details about my spying on the man and finding out that Slurpinthal never turned off his light, and I was pretty sure, never slept. I told Dad about Clara's dreams and about how she believed our neighbor was an alien, too. And then, finally, after I'd blabbed it all out, I stopped and waited for Dad to say something.

At first, I felt kind of guilty for telling him about Clara. We weren't supposed to talk about her . . . talent. But, I'd been trying to give him the whole picture, and everything connected to Slurpinthal, so I'd needed to include that, hadn't I?

We were driving on country roads, tree-lined so that sometimes the leaves sparkled, and sometimes they looked black and evil from the shadows of their shade. The sun was just setting. Its light cast smoky purples across the leafy stretches. The heavy branches that clung to the shadows made the whole place look like tall, thin men reaching out their fingers, ready to grab.

The thought made me shiver, recalling that I still didn't know what Slurpinthal might or might not do about Earthmen — and me, in particular, for spying. I rolled up the window and zipped my sweatshirt jacket to the top.

Dad turned to glance at me and smiled,

"Careful, Kyle, your imagination has started giving you goosebumps."

I suppose I turned red. My face felt suddenly hot, but it might have been only the last rays of the sun striking my cheeks. By then, we were driving through a different patch of road, one by a field with no tall trees.

There was laughter in my father's voice. I suspected that he was making fun of me. It surprised me.

I stared down at my hands. I'd washed them just before we left Bluegrass Farms, but they still looked dirty. My nails had gotten stained from the medicine Dad had used on Painted Starfish. Mom wasn't going to like that. I thought about the kids at school. You could bet someone would see my nails and mock my stained fingernails.

"Hey wheelchair boy, how'd you get your fingernails dirty — doing pushups in beet juice?"

I shut my eyes and told my mind not to imagine things. The stuff I was seeing at school wasn't really happening — not yet, anyway. If you imagined things like that, then it's as if you had to live through it twice. Once was bad enough.

I could feel my dad watching me. He was still laughing a bit, like there were leftover parts he kept turning over to see the funny part underneath.

I checked my nails again, turning them to see if the shadows were playing tricks on me. In the sunshine, they looked worse. I dropped my hands into my lap and stared out the window. If I didn't think about my fingernails, or the way the trees cast their shadows, then all I could concentrate on was the fact that my dad was laughing at me, laughing even though I'd told him the truth.

I remembered that I had my lucky stone in my pocket. I reached in and felt for it. I rubbed it, needing to feel the smoothness of its surface.

I'd given my father as complete a story as I was capable of. I hadn't bounced around or given him surplus data, like Mom called it. Yet, still he was chuckling over my recollections like I'd been making a joke or telling a tall tale.

That hurt. Didn't fathers know that? Didn't they know that a single mean laugh caused more pain than . . . well, than when my doctor injected medication into my spinal column?

I counted trees, trying not to think about it, trying not to hear my father's amusement over what I'd told him.

After a minute, Dad finally sobered, like it had taken him all that time to realize I hadn't joined in. I guess he expected me to double over, snicker, and say, "Oh, Dad, it's only a story I made up. It was funny, right?"

Dad was back on smooth pavement. I'd felt the jerk of it when he'd left the roughness of the back roads. The trees were behind us, too. Instead, there were houses with swing sets in front yards, small plastic pools, flowers, and shrubs. We passed a series of mailboxes. One had a little red flag on the side of the mailbox that was standing at attention. That meant the mailman was supposed to pick up a letter. I knew that because Dad had told me the last time we drove this way.

"Look, Kyle," Dad said when the silence stretched too long. "I know the guy's a little weird. He looks funny and talks funny. But he's not an alien. He was pretty cool about Mom. Most people wouldn't have been that calm to see her fainting away like that. And then when she threw up . . . He handled that well, I must say. Of course, he ate the plant we gave him."

Dad glanced at me again. The traffic was light that day. Dad was holding onto the steering wheel with one hand. His other arm was draped across the seat, his fingers touching my shoulder. Mom would have said something about his casual style of driving.

She always wanted Dad to keep both hands on the steering wheel. But my father was a good driver. He'd never had an accident. Of course, there was a first time for everything, wasn't there? You could even have an accident if you were doing everything right. Look at me. Look at what happened when I relaxed . . .

Chapter Six:

My Sister Clara

No one said anything about my fingernails the next day at school. That was probably because I kept my hands covered most of the day. But maybe it was just that no one looked at me. That happens, you know. Someone in a wheelchair becomes invisible. I guess everyone was trying so hard not to stare, that they forgot that it's okay to say hello, okay to talk, and to invite a wheelchair sitter to join in.

In math class, I didn't do so great on the test. I'd thought I understood, but I didn't. None of my answers matched what was offered. I'd have to get Todd to help me out again. I wished Dad or Mom were good at math, but they were about as useful as asking my five-year-old sister for help.

Mom always said to go find Dad. I think she was afraid of math, although she must do some of it for her business. She was an accountant, wasn't she?

Anyway, so off I'd go to locate my father, but when he tried to help me, he got me so confused, the numbers started to dance, and I'd get even more mixed up than I already was.

In social studies, I made a mistake on my map of Africa and had to start all over again. Then I lost my blue colored pencil. You couldn't do the oceans and lakes without a blue colored pencil. I tried to borrow Theodore's, but he said he needed his.

Frank was using his only blue pencil, too. Wouldn't you know it — the only person who offered to let me use one was Elizabeth. I almost turned her down, not wanting everyone to think she was a friend, but I needed to finish my map. She smiled at me when I borrowed her pencil. How could anyone smile with metal teeth? There ought to be a law against it.

Then, when I gave the pencil back to her, I saw that she was reading a book on horses. I really wanted to talk to her about it, but I didn't. I turned around and pretended I hadn't noticed. I wondered if she really liked horses. Some girls do. Some girls were crazy about them. I bet Elizabeth would like Bay Meadow.

****

After school on Mondays, Wednesdays, and Fridays, I had physical therapy. I guess it sounded strange that I had to go to an exercise class when I really couldn't do much exercising. It's not like I could walk on a treadmill or anything.

I had paraplegia, which meant that my legs didn't function. The accident injured my spinal cord below something called the first thoracic spinal nerve. A doctor told me, right after the accident, that I was lucky. He said if I'd fallen differently, I could have been paralyzed all over — not even able to use my arms and hands.

Sometimes people get frozen everywhere. They can't even smile or laugh or talk. I saw a guy like that in therapy. Only his eyes moved. He was still getting physical therapy, though. They were lifting up his legs and rotating them around, just like they thought he'd walk again someday.

I guess I *was* lucky, but that day when the doctor said it, I didn't think so. I mean, it's not like I was doing something dangerous when I got hurt. I wasn't doing daredevil stuff. I was just riding my bike. Or rather, Clara and I were riding it, because she was on the handlebars.

I hardly ever did that. I knew it wasn't safe, but there were lots of kids who did it all the time. It should have been okay. We would have been fine if that car hadn't swerved into us, and if we hadn't been going over the bridge at Suttor's Creek. If Suttor's Creek hadn't been dry. If . . .

Sorry. That's what my mind does sometimes — it fills up with *ifs*. If only I hadn't done this or that. If only . . .

Anyway, I was talking about my physical therapy session. Barbara — that's what she tells me to call her, even though she's an adult — is really nice. She's pretty, too. I like the way her hair shines like she's always out in the sunshine.

She mostly ties her long blonde hair back into a ponytail, but once I saw her take the rubber band off, and because it was a cold, dry day, her hair had so much static energy, it kept shooting out to the sides, standing up kind of. It looked weird.

With Barbara's help, I use a machine that cycles my legs. My legs can't do it on their own, of course, but the exerciser makes it look like I'm riding a bike. I wish I really could. The doctors want to keep my muscles alive, just in case. Sometimes I think I'm really exercising. I think I might have feeling in my legs, but then the machine gets turned off, and my legs are dead again.

I stare at them and wish them to move, but they don't. It's like there's a disconnect between my brain and legs — like they've forgotten they belong to me. Dr. Pellar says the spinal injections are going to help with that disconnect. He says that my spine's nerves may one day rejuvenate.

Rejuvenate is a word that means to *get fixed*. In the meantime, I have to remind my muscles what it's like to do things. I guess they'd forget how to ride a bike or walk without the therapy.

Barbara hooks me up to another machine that sends electricity through my legs. It doesn't hurt, but she has to put goop on them. I don't like that part, but at least she wipes the goop off when it's all finished. The electricity just feels warm, at least, that's what Barbara says. I'm not sure I can even feel it.

I know that sounds strange. One ought to be able to say they can feel things or not feel them, but my legs play tricks on me. One day I thought I had a cramp in my leg. It hurt something awful. Mom rushed me to the hospital because I was crying. But there was nothing wrong. It was only my imagination.

I think that's what Dr. Pillar said. He called it psychosomatic. I don't understand why I'd want to imagine having a pain. It really felt like it hurt. But after they x-rayed my leg and did a whole bunch of tests, they couldn't find anything wrong. Then the pain stopped. It was like someone had suddenly turned off my pain switch. Really weird, right?

That's why I say that I *think* I feel things, rather than I feel them. I'm never sure anymore. Dr. Pillar says that psychosomatic pain might be a good thing, that maybe it means my legs are responsive. I hope so, but I think it's odd to think that something that hurts that much could be a good thing.

Barbara gives me cool massages. She makes me lie on my stomach and then presses on my back. Mom and Dad joke that they'd like her to give them a massage, too. The best part is not that Barbara is relaxing my muscles, as she puts it, but that she talks to me while she does it.

She likes to tell me about movies she's seen and books she's read. Sometimes she asks me questions, but I really can't talk while she's giving me a massage. For one thing, the pressure she's applying to my back makes my speech come out in grunts, and for another, my mouth is usually pressed against the brown rubber mat of the table she has me lying on. Anything I say is mumbled, so she has to ask me to repeat it several times. That's why I'd just rather listen to her talk. I really like to listen to what she says.

The physical therapy room smells. There's a faint sweat odor, but it's not that bad. Mostly it smells like menthol — you know the stuff in cough drops. They use some kind of menthol cream on us that's supposed to help the muscles.

Barbara has a smell, too. It's a fragrance that reminds me of flowers. I think it's only the shampoo she uses, but I like Barbara's smell. I just try not to let her see me inhaling deeply when she leans over me or gets real close.

The waiting room stinks. The secretary put a huge potted plant in there that's always getting watered while I'm there. The plant makes the room smell like rotting bananas. That's what I think, but Mom says it's my imagination. She thinks the room smells fine. It's a good thing she thinks that. She has to stay there a long time.

Usually she does her work on a little laptop, but sometimes she reads magazines. Mom says she doesn't mind waiting there, but when she sees me come out, there's always such a look of relief on her face that I know she really doesn't like waiting for me. Maybe she really thinks the room smells like rotten bananas, but just doesn't want to admit it.

When I got out of therapy on Wednesday, as Mom and I were walking out into the parking lot of the Steven K. Gershwin Medical Facility, I saw Slurpinthal. He was heading the other way, so it was only the back of him, but I'm sure it was him. The person I saw was the same height, had the same funny gait as him, and was wearing bright purple shoes. I pointed him out to Mom, but she didn't see him. She was talking on the phone and wasn't paying attention.

I repeated my words, tugging at her arm. But when she finally listened and looked, Slurpinthal was out of sight. Even after Mom finally heard me, she didn't seem all that interested. She was worried about Dad not having picked up Clara from the preschool.

I know I saw Slurpinthal, but what was he doing at the Medical Facility? Did aliens visit doctors? Was there physical therapy for flying saucer men?

I wondered if I should have called out to him. Would he have stopped and looked back? Would he have had a normal conversation with us? Or would he have pretended he didn't know us?

Maybe he was doing something secret, something he didn't want us to know about. Maybe he was trying to learn about human anatomy so he could take over the world. Did he need something from the hospital complex? Was he visiting Earth merely for research?

Maybe he worked there. What did Slurpinthal do for a living? I'd never seen him outside his house before. I asked Mom if she knew where our neighbor worked, but she said she didn't know. That could have meant anything — like she was just too busy to remember what she'd heard. I mean, wasn't that always the first thing adults found out about each other? Hi, my name is Mrs. So and So. I work at Sandpit Construction or whatever. For kids, it was always how old we were and what grade we were in. Adults peg people by jobs. Kids sort out each other by classrooms.

Mom was still on the phone talking to Dad. She was angry sounding, her voice louder and shriller than usual. I wondered if that's what Todd heard all the time. It hurt my stomach. It made me sick inside to hear Mom use that tone with Dad, like I was going to shrink down inside myself and disappear into nothingness. Kissing and handholding were so much better than jolts of rage.

Thankfully, it only lasted a minute, though. Then Mom was opening the door of the car, and we were heading over to the preschool to pick up Clara.

I suppose you're wondering why a five year old had to go to pre-school. It wasn't because they thought she wouldn't be able to keep up. Clara was anything but slow. She was, in fact, super bright, according to what I overheard Mom telling Dad.

My parents had taken Clara to a psychiatrist to make sure she was okay, if you know what I mean. That was when Clara started predicting things, and my parents got worried about it. The doctor ran some tests. He told them that everything was okay with Clara's mind. He assured them she wasn't crazy, just imaginative. In fact, the doctor said she was gifted which meant that my little sister was "highly intelligent," which is how the doctor put it.

I could have told my parents that. Clara was strange in some ways — like the way she treated her doll like it was real, and having nightmares so often probably wasn't normal, but foretelling the future, that was cool. Clara could already read books, books without pictures, and she hadn't even started real school yet. So it was obvious the psychiatrist was right about her brain power.

Anyway, even though she was officially five years old, Clara still couldn't go to kindergarten because she missed the cut-off. Her birthday was too late, by three days. Weird, huh? That's just like with horses. All of the foals turn one year old on January 1st, even if they were just born a month before. It's a really strict rule if the horses are thoroughbreds that race on the track.

But apparently, kindergarten was like the horse racing industry. It probably didn't matter much for Clara. What was she going to learn in public school kindergarten that she couldn't learn in preschool? She already knew how to read. She could print her name, her numbers, and even do a bunch of math. (Maybe in a few years she could be my math tutor?)

I thought that next year Clara should skip kindergarten and go right to first grade, but the psychiatrist said she shouldn't. He said she needed the socialization of kindergarten. What did he think she was doing in pre-school?

That day, when we arrived at the preschool building, Clara was the last kid to be picked up. She wasn't worried, though. She was curled up in the big red bean bag, reading a book. When we came in, Clara didn't even look up. She didn't "hear" us until Mom called out, "Clara."

Then my sister sighed, closed the book without any marker, and holding it in her hand as if it were as important as her silly Babydoll, she picked up her backpack, and walked over to us. Clara hardly ever ran. She always says that people miss *seeing* when they run, whatever that means.

Clara was never teary-eyed about being picked up or dropped off at school. Some of the kids cried for half an hour due to what the teacher called *abandonment issues*. Not Clara. She accepted arrivals and departures with the calmness of an older child. (I once overheard her teacher explaining to Mom that Clara's composure was quite rare for a child in pre-school. I later found out that composure is like being at peace. That's Clara, all right, except when she had nightmares.)

Seeing me, Clara's face produced a great, big smile. She and I usually got along pretty well. We had to, since I was the one who ended up babysitting her in the middle of the night. I smiled back and jerked on one of her braids. Of course, I didn't do it to hurt her. Clara always thought my braid tugging was funny. She giggled, then darted a kiss at my cheek.

But Mom never remembered that. She scolded me whenever she saw me reach for Clara's hair. Mom often lectured me about being nice to my sister, too, whenever she thought about it. That day she didn't notice my quick braid tug. She was still fuming because Dad hadn't picked Clara up.

When Dad got home that evening, Mom wouldn't speak to him. Dinner tasted bland. None of us wanted to swallow. Even the milk tasted off. Clara and I didn't bother sticking around. We passed on dessert. After we left the table, Clara hopped up the stairs to her room, holding one foot in her hand — even though Mom always tells her not to do that. She tells Clara that she should hold on to the rail so she didn't fall, but Clara was always doing weird stuff as she climbed.

It was a really good thing that Mom didn't know about some of the other daredevil things Clara did, like standing on her hands, although that didn't last more than the bottom three steps, or pretending she was blind, or going up the stairs backwards.

I think Clara was excited about getting to read more of her book. That night, she didn't even wait at the top of the staircase to stick out her tongue at me. Instead, she went hopping into her room and quietly closed the door. Most of the time, after the tongue bit, when she reached the top, she did the caterpillar crawl or the crab walk. She'd explained once that cartwheels made too much noise, and Mom always yelled when she did them in the house.

I rode the elevator up, headed for my room, and started in on my homework immediately. Downstairs, I could hear Mom and Dad washing the dishes. They always did dishes together during the week because Clara and I had homework. (Not that Clara really had homework, but she always pretended that she did.)

On the weekend, Clara and I did clean up, and my parents watched T.V. together. They sat close to each other, sort of hugging. Clara and I sometimes spied on them, but that's what all kids do, right?

That night, I kept my door open to listen to my parents, but I didn't hear any shouting. Even when my parents were mad at each other, I'd never heard them argue. Yet, knowing what had happened with Todd's parents, I worried that there could always be a first time, a day when they would get so furious with each other, one of them might leave.

I needed to be prepared for that, just in case. But, if it did happen, I'd go down and try to stop the parent who was trying to leave. I'd even plead the "I'm a poor boy in a wheelchair excuse, so they'd be guilt-tripped into staying.

I think angry adults should talk about their problems. They should say, "When you stepped on my foot, it hurt. In the future, would you please not step on my foot?" That was what we practiced at school. After we said that, everything was okay.

It worked especially well for hurt feelings. I wished Dad and Mom would try it. Then they could say they were sorry and go out and play. How come things were so simple in school and so complicated everywhere else?

That night when Dad came into my room to say goodnight, I asked him how it was going. He told me that everything was all right again. He said that he and Mom would never get a divorce and that he didn't want to move out, either. That was a good conversation to go to sleep on. I'm sure I was smiling when I nodded off.

Chapter Seven:

A Strange Light in the Sky

Something woke me up in the middle of the night. I thought at first that Clara was having another nightmare. She was. I could hear her softly crying, the way she did when she was still asleep but deep in a horrible dream. But, she hadn't reached the point where she needed me to calm her down yet.

I didn't think it was her sniffles that woke me up. I was pretty sure it was the strange light in the sky. Even from my bed, I could see a rainbow out my window. I mean, it was dark and not rainy at all, but yet over near Simon's house, there was a moon-shaped rainbow.

I guess that didn't make sense. Rainbows had arcs. They couldn't be round. But what I saw was spherical, and multi-colored. I guess it was kind of like the strobe lights they have at roller skating rinks, but not as shiny and much, much bigger.

I pulled the wheelchair close and lifted my body into it. Then I pushed myself toward the window. Behind me, I could hear Clara's whimpers. I needed to go to her, but I couldn't yet. I had to get closer to that ball of rainbow lights. I had to see what was holding it up.

The Simon's window was all lit up, but I didn't think anything of it. The light was always on in Slurpinthal's room. I noticed that his window was open, though. That was unusual. I reached up and opened mine. Mom would get mad if she knew. She always warned us not to open our windows when the air conditioning was on in the summer and the heater was going in the winter.

Even though we weren't using either of those that night, I knew Mom still wouldn't like me hanging out of the window into the darkness, but something was ordering me to do it. Something was making me reach up and slide the window toward the left.

"What are you doing?" Clara asked.

My hand froze. I turned to look at her.

"What are you doing out of bed?"

Seeing her reaction to my question sickened me. I realized I sounded like Mom.

"Sorry," I added, and she nodded her head and moved closer.

Plopping down on the foot of my bed, she asked, "Why did you open the window? It was in my dream. You fell. You fell out of the window."

There were tears on her cheeks. I rolled nearer. "I wasn't going to fall, Clara. I wouldn't do that."

She was quietly sobbing. I put my hand on her shoulder, just a pat, just a friendly *I am there.*

"What are you two doing up?" my mother cried out as she turned on the light.

My sister, tears smeared across her face, was sobbing into her hands. I was sitting in my wheelchair with the window open. Everything was pretty obvious, but of course, I couldn't say that to my mother.

"She had a bad dream, Mom," I said, babbling out the first thing that came to my mind. Of course, that kind of laid it in Clara's ballpark, but she was the one crying.

"Oh, I see," Mom said. Her eyes fluttered about the room. They took in the open window.

"Shut that," Mom demanded. Then she turned on her heels and went back to bed.

That left me open-mouthed. She hadn't even asked about Clara's dream. Nor had she wanted to know why I'd opened the window. I suppose there are some who question a gift horse, but I'm not one of them. I returned to the window and slid it closed. Then I turned to look at my sister. She wasn't crying anymore. She was laughing.

"What?" I asked, shaking my head because I couldn't understand either my mother or my sister.

"Don't you see?" she said. "We were supposed to do this. It was part of the dream. I thought you fell, but you didn't. I remember that now. I came into your room, and you turned to talk to me. Then Mom came in, and . . . It was all in my dream like that, only I didn't remember. I'm so glad, Kyle. That means I saved you. In my dream and now."

I stared out the window, listening, thinking about what she was saying. If it had been anyone else saying those things, I would have shrugged my shoulders and gone to bed, but Clara knew the future. Clara was special. Did she mean that Slurpinthal wanted me dead?

"No, Kyle. It wasn't him. It was someone else. Someone else was making you open that window. I don't know who. Someone horrible with a face like . . ."

She didn't finish. I looked back and saw that she was crying again. Just like that. Laughing one moment, and then crying.

"Clara, it's okay. No one's here. You saved me, remember. Don't cry."

Her eyes, when she looked up at me, were kind of scary-looking — all red in the white part, with pupils huge and dark. If I'd been a painter, the way her eyes looked that moment is exactly how I would have painted FEAR.

"Look, we've both got school in the morning. Can you sleep now?"

Clara shook her head. I should have known. Dumb me. Of course, she couldn't sleep. She was still shaking. I yawned. I was the one who wanted to go to bed. Not Clara. She was still recoiling from the scary guy in her dreams. I was glad I hadn't seen him, glad I hadn't dreamed about him, anyway.

"Listen, we do have to sleep, Clara. Get under the covers. I'll just take the top blanket and curl up in my chair. Okay?"

"I can stay here?" she asked, her eyes even wider with disbelief.

"Sure, and we'll keep the lights on too. That way nothing can get in to disturb us."

Clara nodded. She scurried under the covers. I realized that part of her shivers hadn't been from fear, but from cold. As she shifted down into my warm and comfortable bed, I grabbed a blanket and tried to find comfort.

The moon was hanging low, practically right outside my window, or at least it looked like that. But our moon wasn't the sphere with colors that I'd seen earlier. No rainbows grinned from the center of its dark shadows. But it still loomed there, too close for comfort.

I stared at the real moon a while, thinking about the night. I suppose I shifted about in my chair, squeezing parts of my body into more comfortable positions. My elbows felt strange, for some reason.

They seemed bigger and more angular. I kept moving them, trying to find the place where they fit. I must have fallen asleep worrying over my elbows because in the morning, when Clara jiggled my arm to wake me up, my elbows were all stiff and out of sorts. I groaned.

"You okay?" she asked.

I nodded, not wanting her to see that I was all needles and pins. That's exactly what I felt like — like someone had jabbed me with needles all about my body.

Clara didn't know that, of course. She skipped away, singing her favorite song, *Tomorrow*.

I watched her leave. When she shut the door behind her, I groaned out loudly. Then I made my way into the bathroom, where I took a long hot shower as I sat on my plastic chair in the corner of the stall. After a good tooth brushing, a swift hair management session, and an inspection to see if I was growing a mustache yet, I wheeled myself back into my room and began sorting through my clothes. That day was an orange day at school. What a dreadful color. I hated school spirit day.

As I was getting dressed in an old orange t-shirt that had a picture of our school mascot, the cougar, I peeked out through my dark blue drapes to see what the weather was like. A motion from across the way caught my eye. Slurpinthal was leaning out his window, staring over at my room. I retreated quickly — I think before he saw me. My heart was flip-flopping. My knees started quivering. What was Slurpinthal doing? Why was he staring over at my room?

The rain started during breakfast. I'd thought it was supposed to be sunny, but the clouds had blown in roughly, seizing the trees and shaking them. From the breakfast table, it sounded like a hurricane.

Mom chugged her coffee, made a quick call, and said, "Let's go, kids. Looks like I've got to drop you off today."

I started to ask about Dad, but then I remembered. He'd gone out in the night. Mom had told me he was with a sick stallion, Mr. Foster's prize Clydesdale. Snowdrop, named for the snowflake-like white patch on his forehead, was a pussycat even though standing next to him felt like standing beside a giant elephant. He was nearly that big. He had huge feet that were feathered with hair. Each of his hooves was about the size of a dinner plate. If he ever stepped on you, you'd have a foot flatter than a swim flipper.

I followed Mom to the window. I hadn't finished my cereal, but I wanted to see what the weather was doing. Did it look as bad as it sounded?

Mom gave me a look, but she didn't scold. She just patted me on the shoulder, sighed heavily, and said, "Put your dishes in the sink, Kyle. Can you help Clara?"

I nodded. I was watching the branches bob up and down with the gusts of wind. Rain was falling like cats and dogs — an expression I'd always wondered about. Why not sheep and goats? Or — because of all that water, wouldn't ducks and swans be better?

I walked back to the table, picked up my bowl and glass and, since Mom had left the room, slurped down the rest of my milk and cereal using the bowl as my cup. Clara laughed and did the same. She wasn't as neat about it, though. Milk ran down the front of her shirt and slopped onto the table.

"Clara!" I hissed.

She handed me the now empty bowl and giggled, shrugging her shoulders. Then she lifted up Babydoll. "It was her fault, you know, Kyle. She was laughing at me."

"Put on your raincoat," I said, bossily. "If you cover-up, Mom won't see the mess you made."

71

Actually, Clara's shirt was pretty wet. I felt guilty as I mopped up the mess with the extension sponge (something Dad had rigged up, which was merely a sponge tied to the end of a long stick). Clara's little act of rebellion had made a mess all over the floor as well as the table, but a couple of swabs here and there fixed it completely. I cocked my head, studied my sister, and then helped her zip up her raincoat.

I thought about taking the elevator up to her room to grab another shirt, but Mom would hear me for sure. Then it hit me, there was always laundry on top of the dryer. I wheeled my chair into the laundry room, grabbed a clean shirt, and returned just in time to stuff it into Clara's backpack before Mom came tearing in to say, "Hurry, kids, Let's go."

I slipped my rain poncho over my head and headed for the door. At least Dad and the sick Clydesdale could stay inside the horse's nice warm stable. Clara, Mom, and I were going to have to wade through several big puddles just to get to our car.

As usual, Mom started mumbling about our lack of garage. Dad had taken ours over to create a veterinarian's office for his bookkeeping and supplies. Now we had to park our cars on the gravel driveway. Poor Mom. Her heels were sinking.

Mom slid into the car, then worked the hydraulic that lifted me up into the vehicle. I probably could have dragged myself. Thanks to the exercises I did at physical therapy, my arms were getting really strong. However, I still couldn't lift the wheelchair up into the van. Besides, Mom was always afraid I'd fall out trying to grab it.

I hated waiting for the lever to shift through its gears. The rain falling on my umbrella was pounding with a steady beat. The air was cold and damp. It felt like winter was back again, although we'd been having spring-like days.

Inside the van, it was warm. Mom had the heater going full blast. Clara started to unzip her raincoat. I shook my head and warned her not to with my eyes. Thankfully, again, Mom didn't notice anything strange. She was shifting the car into reverse, eager to back out of our long, skinny driveway.

Slurpinthal was walking out to visit his mailbox. We all waved to him, but either he didn't see us, or he didn't want to respond. He was staring at a box, shoved halfway into the mailbox. Of course, it was getting drenched. If he cared so much about whatever had been delivered, he should have picked it up the day before. Our mailman usually came around 9:00 o'clock in the morning. That meant the package had sat in the mailbox all day yesterday and throughout the night.

As Mom drove us out onto the road, I kept my eyes on Slurpinthal. He was tugging at the package. The last I saw, it had ripped in half, part of it still stuck inside the mailbox. A giant flash of lightning caused my mom to swerve. Thunder rumbled almost the next moment.

"I don't think it's safe to drive," Mom said, as she pulled over to the side of the road. It was lucky she did. The rain chose that moment to release a whole cloud's worth of water. It fell as if the cloud was a water trough or a bathtub someone had tipped over.

"Are we going to drown?" Clara asked, sounding more curious than scared.

Mom and I shook our heads, laughing, but I caught Mom giving Clara a funny look, as if she wondered what Clara knew.

"Any dreams about rainy days?" Mom tossed the question out as if it held no significance, but I knew she was asking about forewarnings.

"Only that there was a leak in Mr. Slurpinthal's bathroom," Clara told her without batting an eye. "But it's okay, really. The water falls nicely into his bathtub. He doesn't use it anyway."

Again, I started laughing, but Mom's eyes warned me to be quiet. Apparently, she wasn't done with her probing. "That's all, right, Clara. But no dreams about anything else? Daddy's fine, and . . ."

Clara looked up from playing with Babydoll. As I'd said before, she's not a stupid girl. Her eyes began to twinkle. "I think I remember something bad. I think we should all stay home and make cookies today."

The rain that a moment ago had been fierce enough to rock the car now issued a gentler pounding sound. Mom shook her head. "Clara, no cookies. We have school and work today, remember?"

As Mom started the engine, the rain lightened even more. The windshield wipers started to squeak. Mom turned them down and drove forward.

I know that doesn't sound like an important conversation to relate. I mean, thunder and lightning are cool, and the fact that Mom relied on Clara's visions was kind of interesting, but that's not why I told you about it. I have my reasons. They have something to do with what happened later that night when we were all snug and warm inside our house.

School was normal — for a rainy day, anyway. Rain at school meant that we couldn't go outside and play, but I rarely did anyway, so that part wasn't really any different. The high concentration of creeps is what was bothersome. Most of them usually went outside to kick a ball around, or each other, I suppose, since they were constantly getting into fights. (I know because they usually came in late with a note from the office, and our teacher always said, "Not again. When are you going to learn that you can't hit at school?")

On rainy days, trapped inside, those kinds of guys hunted for fresh meat. Guess who always happened to fit the bill? Of course, they didn't hit or kick me, although it was fair game to knock my books off the desk or to pick up my lunch and cart it away. It was also unobservable (at least to the teacher's notice) if they passed a note with a stupid drawing on it that made me look all skinny and long nosed.

They always managed after a period of giggling (Yes, guys giggle. I'd observed it often.) to drop the note on top of my things or even to mix it in with my papers. Twice, they've planted it in my sweatshirt hood. I don't wear anything with a hood anymore for that reason. Anyway, the taunting was all normal stuff that I just had to endure until I got through school, or the boys became more human.

Todd and I sat together and talked during lunch recess. His father was moving out again. This time he said his father was going to find an apartment. That sounded more serious than spending a week in a hotel.

Todd's eyes looked saggy as he talked. His face had broken out, too. He had a pimple on the right side of his chin. Of course, I didn't mention it. I just listened as he told me that his mom was at home and had called in sick. Todd said she was all red-eyed and drippy-nosed.

I could tell that Todd was worried that she might be drinking again. She used to hide dark brown bottles of alcohol in the hamper and under the bathroom sink. Todd had begun searching for them again.

I offered to let Todd stay with us. I felt guilty that I hadn't asked my mom and dad first, but it didn't matter because Todd shook his head and said, "I can't. I need to watch her, you know. I've got to try to stop her from . . ."

His eyes grew teary. He looked away and didn't finish his sentence. I stared up at the map on the wall that showed the mountain ranges of North and South America. It was an old map, faded from years of use. Someone had written something on the right side, but I couldn't read it. I think the teacher tried to erase it once, but only tore the map. The cities were once marked with red dots, but they looked pink now. They reminded me of the pimple on Todd's chin.

And then I was suddenly staring at the tear. It seemed to ripple, to move as if something lay beneath it. Todd saw my concentration, and although a moment before he couldn't stop rubbing his saddened eyes, he stopped and peered at the map.

"What is it?" he asked. 'What are you staring at?"

I started to reply. Surely he must have seen the way the paper peeled back, revealing the wall behind it, a wall that showed a diagram of a spaceship. Why didn't he mention it?

I started to ask him that, to grab at his sleeve and jerk him into recognition, but then I realized the map wasn't moving anymore. The wall beneath it wasn't visible. There was no spaceship.

Was I going mad? Was I becoming like Clara, clairvoyant? I shook my head, looked down at my hands, and mentally ironed out my face.

"Nothing," I said because Todd was still staring at me.

Two seats over, one of the creep heads was staring, too. He was laughing and punching his friend. Both of them were watching me. I tried not to notice them, but from the corner of my eye I saw a long, thin stick — like a fishing pole. That's when it hit me that they were taunting me again, trying to see if I'd freak out or respond in some other way so they could jeer and laugh over my idiocy.

"Never mind, Todd. It was just the clowns," I said. Then I turned my wheelchair about so my back was to them. I didn't want to see their faces as mine boiled and probably darkened to a shade somewhat like a rotting tomato and putrid with hate.

****

At home that evening, my father regaled us with tales of the Clydesdale. I laughed, forgetting how miserable I'd been. The rain was still falling. The wind kept howling and swishing. The tree in the front bowed and creaked, whipping its branches about as if it were alive and quarreling violently with the wind.

I remembered seeing Native Americans in an old Western. The chief kept bobbing his head up and down, in a rain dance. His feathered headdress kept time with the movement of his feet.

Poor tree. No rain dance for it, but the tree acted like it wanted to rip the soil and pull up its roots so it could bob and spin about like the dancing chief.

Dad was telling us about how the giant horse looked like he was crying when Dad put the dab of iodine on its leg. The silly horse had scraped his hock on a roughened side of the stall. The old stallion liked to rub against the stone wall, pressing hard enough to take off skin. Dad had wormed the animal, he told us, just to be sure that wasn't the cause of his problem, but he told us that he doubted the stallion was anything but bored.

"Let him gallop about the pasture now and then," Dad had told the farmer, but the man had looked so shocked Dad told us he worried he'd have to give the man some smelling salts to keep him from fainting.

"He's a horse, Ben," Dad had told the farmer. "He needs a good run."

According to Dad, the farmer just shook his head. "This is a prize-winning stallion. He can't go for wild gallops anymore. He has to be walked so he doesn't hurt himself, except I can't take him out anymore, and he's too much of a handful for my son. Snowdrop needs a firm and very strong hand. He forgets he's getting old when he gets outside."

Dad said that the farmer reached over then and whacked the horse on the flank, making Dad jump, but Snowdrop only nickered and rubbed his head on his owner's shirt. Snowdrop knew he was being praised.

"It's a real shame about that animal," my dad told us. "A horse like that ought to be sent out to pasture to end his days, not be cooped up like a bird in a cage. The stall is plenty big, but that's still not enough. He's got a little paddock outside, too, so he can feel the sunshine on his bones, but a horse like that . . ."

A knock on the door ended my dad's words. He glanced at us, looked down at his unfinished dinner, sighed, and stood up.

Chapter Eight:

Smashing Carrots

Now, who could that be on a night like this?" Mom asked after watching Dad get up and head for the front door.

Clara poked one of the *nibble carrots*, as we called them, into her mouth, and while she was chewing, said, "It's Slurpinthal, of course."

Normally, Mom would have been all over Clara about talking with her mouth full, but Mom didn't say a word. She just stood up and went to join my father.

"Are you sure?" I asked my sister.

Clara ate another nibble carrot and munched happily while nodding her head. "He's here about his roof. He wants to know what to do."

We could hear the sound of talking, but we really couldn't make out what the adults were saying. It didn't matter. Mom and Dad returned to the dining room, dragging Slurpinthal with them. Dad motioned to Slurpinthal to take a seat. Clara stuffed another carrot into her mouth. Then she handed the bowl to Slurpinthal.

He looked from my sister to my parents. Then he glanced at me. I hadn't eaten my carrots. They were on my plate. I picked up one and started nibbling. Apparently, that was enough for Slurpinthal. He grabbed a handful and put them all in his mouth.

The alien must have really good teeth. That many carrots is difficult to chew, but Slurpinthal crunched them like they were soft and easy to chomp. He ground them up with no apparent embarrassment at the loudness of the process, either. If you want to know what it sounded like, listen to a garbage disposal grinding up a cup of carrots — same pulverizing grinds, gurgles, and chomps.

Dad sat down to finish his meal. Mom ran into the kitchen to get Slurpinthal a plate. She slipped it in front of him, but he didn't seem to notice. He was eyeing the carrots, although his mouth was still full of chopped pieces.

Clara moved the bowl closer to him, and again Slurpinthal reached in and took out a handful. Only this time, discovering his plate, he grinned widely, placed the carrots onto his plate, and grabbed another handful. Trying not watch, I noticed that he mostly emptied the bowl. Mom would have to buy more the next day. That amount usually lasted us a full week.

Neither Mom nor Dad said anything, though. They were delighted that Slurpinthal had come over. Neighborly-like, they were probably thinking. I wondered what the alien was up to. Was the leak in his roof the only reason he was visiting us?

When we were finished, Dad got up and took away our plates. He left Slurpinthal's, though. The alien was still munching away, grinning happily with little bits of carrot in his slightly orange-tinted teeth. Clara and I watched him as he plopped carrot after carrot into his mouth. It was like feeding a food processor, dropping things down the hole, piece by piece.

Even though Slurpinthal was making his garbage disposer noise, I could still hear the wind beating against the house. Great roars were rising and falling, making the front yard sound like a herd of lions had taken up residence. The biggest tree continued its rain dance, although still stuck in place. The smaller bushes were just shaking their heads back and forth, as if none of them agreed with what was happening. The rain kept throwing itself at all the grasses and plants, trampling everything green, no doubt turning hardened gravel and dirt into pools and eddies of swamp water.

I wondered if I'd be able to push my wheelchair down the driveway in the morning. Would Mom be able to back the van out of the sodden driveway? I started to ask Slurpinthal how he'd gotten over to our house, but I knew he'd walked. He didn't seem to own a vehicle, at least, not the kind that Earth people knew about.

When Mom and Dad returned, Slurpinthal was just finishing the last of his carrots. He hadn't wanted anything else that we'd offered him. He passed over the meatloaf, the green peas, the gravy, and the mashed potatoes. Only the carrots seemed to light up his smile. Gross, if you asked me.

Apparently, Mom had stopped at the store that day because she was carrying a big chocolate cake. Dad brought in little saucers and fresh forks. Slurpinthal eyed the cake. His head tilted slightly. His mouth opened and closed. Small bits of carrots dropped onto his shirt, but he didn't notice. He was too busy staring at the plate in Mom's hands.

"What is?" Slurpinthal asked with almost the same enthusiasm he'd shown for the carrots.

My mother kind of blushed. I don't know why. She hadn't made the cake, yet she seemed unsure about her answer. She hesitated for a moment long enough for my father to step in.

"Neither of us do a lot of baking these days. We splurged on a cake today — from the grocery store. Do you like chocolate?"

"Grocery store? Oh, this is to eat?" Slurpinthal's face paled. He turned away without answering Dad and checked to see if there were any carrots left. Fortunately, there were. He scooped out the rest, piling them onto his plate.

"Good. Carrots good," he said, looking at me as if I'd been about to say something.

Had I known what to say, carrots wouldn't have been my topic of conversation. I wanted to ask him what he was doing at our house, what he was doing on Earth, and especially, why he'd tried to kill me the night before.

Perhaps he was somewhat telepathic. He stopped chewing for a moment and turned to search my eyes.

"I. No. Ball entreats only."

My father's eyes were bulging out of their sockets as he tried to make sense of that. Clara's eyes widened to twice their usual size. Mom, perhaps thinking about work and not really listening to what was going on around her, began cutting the cake, whistling in a rather tuneless manner.

Slurpinthal's eyes flip-flopped from Dad to Clara to my mother, and then back to me.

"Ball entreats but not malicious."

I wasn't sure what malicious meant. I glanced at Dad.

"A malicious ball?" he roared. "Has Kyle been throwing balls at your house? Is that what you mean?"

I shook my head and cried out, "I never . . ." but Dad waved me silent.

"Speak up, Mr. Slurpinthal. If either of my children bothers you in some way, then you must tell me immediately. They are good children. They are not allowed to harass people."

The lightning was back. It thundered overhead with a great clap of anger. The lights flickered twice. You could hear something making chtttch sounds, like a sprinkler, except more ominous. Deep inside me, I knew it was the sound of a wire fizzing before it burst into flame.

I straightened up in my chair, dropped my hands to the wheels, and prepared to rush out of the house, if I needed to. I think we all tensed like that, but no one moved because at that moment the lights went out, and we found ourselves totally in the dark. Mom screamed, and Dad said, "Everyone, stay calm."

Clara's hand found mine. I took it and pulled her closer. I could feel her body shaking. What was she afraid of? What was she sensing? She couldn't fear there'd be any danger from Mr. Slurpinthal. At the first sound of lightning, he'd ducked under the table. He was cowering under it. Not that I could see him. But I could hear. The man was whimpering like a frightened puppy.

Dad found a flashlight and shone the light on everyone as if counting heads. "Where's Mr. Slurpinthal?" he demanded as if I or my sister had done something awful to him.

I pointed under the table. Dad got down on his knees and shone the light on our neighbor.

"It's alright, Mr. Slurpinthal. There's probably just a pole down somewhere, or perhaps a transformer has blown. They'll fix it soon. I'll go see if I can find our old camping gear. I have an old battery lamp. We can use that until the electricity comes back on."

Mr. Slurpinthal didn't look up. His whimpers continued.

"They're coming," Clara said.

The voice came from her, but it didn't sound like my sister. It sounded hollow or something. I stared down at her, watching her eyes.

"What does she mean?" my mom asked.

Dad had taken the light away. It was dark in the living room except when the lightning lit up the sky. Thunder boomed almost instantly after.

"It's close," Mom said.

"They're coming," Clara said again.

And then someone knocked at the door.

Clara screamed. Mr. Slurpinthal whimpered louder. I felt my knees buckle. I wet my lips and wiped the sweat off my forehead. As I did, Mom rushed over to the front door and opened it.

Aliens are supposed to be green, I think you know. They're supposed to be clothed in silver or gold. I've always imagined them to have six long, skinny fingers and noses either shorter or longer than ours. I never imagined that they'd be wearing business suits and look like everyone else.

Three men entered the house, waving a badge at Mom. That's why she didn't slam the door in their faces. That's why when they ordered her to do so, she took them into the dining room where the rest of us were. Of course, Dad wasn't there. He was still down in the basement rummaging around for the lantern.

When the men entered, Slurpinthal stopped sniveling. In fact, he didn't make a sound, as if he were hiding from them, as if . . .

The men demanded that we turn on the lights. Not waiting for Mom to comply, one of them rushed over to the switch and began working it up and down. Of course that didn't have any effect, but the man kept doing it over and over.

Mom's face no longer looked friendly. Her eyes held warning lights and were squinting, a sure sign she was angry. She was biting her lip, too, which she only did when something was bothering her. One of the business suits had shown Mom an I.D. card, so Mom had introduced them as officers of the law, but the suits didn't look like policemen. The men had heavy eyebrows, overly narrow lips, and frowns that made them look mean as the Billy goat one of the neighbors kept tied to a stake.

"Kyle," Mom whispered. "Take Clara and go into the kitchen, please."

I wanted to see what was going to happen. I wanted to know if the men had come for Slurpinthal, but I heard the worry in Mom's voice and retreated slowly, pulling Clara with me.

"They are here," she said. "I knew they were coming. They are here," she whispered, leaning against me, almost climbing into my lap.

"Sh," I said.

The kitchen was even darker than the dining room. It had a window that looked out into the front yard. But that wall was attached to the garage, so that half the window peered into the darkness of an enclosed office, one filled with boxes, horse blankets, and veterinarian gear.

"They have come for Slurpinthal," Clara whispered. "Don't let them take him, okay?"

I wished I could have seen Clara's face at that moment. I wanted to ask questions about what she was thinking, why she'd suddenly adopted our strange, alien neighbor, and why she thought I could do anything to protect him, but I didn't dare speak.

Mom was out there with those men, the ones that I didn't think were really policemen. Would they hurt her? Would they drag Slurpinthal out from under the table and cart him away? What did they want with him? And equally significant, what would happen when Dad finally came back upstairs with the lantern?

Clara let go of my hand and moved away. I grabbed at her, but she darted out of my reach. What was she doing?

"Don't go back in there," I said. "Mom wants you to stay here."

Clara didn't answer, but I heard her step behind me, not toward the dining room. Clara was heading to the cabinet where Mom kept her pots and pans.

"Be quiet," I said. "Don't . . ."

It was too late. She'd already pulled out several pans. They clanged as they hit each other. Surely the men would hear the noise. They'd be coming any minute. I wheeled my chair toward her, grabbed her shirt, and headed for the garage door. Clara, strangely, didn't struggle, but she held onto the three pans she'd grabbed. I opened the door, and we scooted into Dad's office.

"We can hide behind the boxes," I said.

But Clara wasn't listening. Her hands walked the wall, allowing her to walk into the pitch dark. Of course, I was right behind her, holding onto her t-shirt. Clara was my responsibility. I wasn't going to let her get herself captured by those men. I'd fight them with shoe leather and finger nails, if needed.

In that way, hugging the wall, walking with hesitation on our tiptoes so we were extra quiet, we made it to the other side of the garage. Then Clara put down the three pots she'd carried with her and began digging among Dad's things. What was she looking for? I suddenly realized her intent. She'd found a flashlight. How had she known it was there?

"Don't turn it on," I hissed, but her hands were already cranking it. It took no more than twenty seconds before a pale light issued from one end. I turned to face the door into the house. I couldn't hear anyone coming. Maybe it was okay. Maybe they wouldn't see the tiny light. But if they followed the noise of the pots and pans, I knew they might see the light. They would probably see us, too.

I pushed my wheelchair deeper between the boxes and waved my hand for Clara to do the same. She stopped cranking, let the light die out, and retreated into our new hiding place. Even I couldn't see her, and I still had my hand on her shirt.

It was a good thing we'd extinguished the light, because just as that moment, the door flew open and two of the men stood glaring into the darkness of the room.

"Do you see the kiddlings?" one asked the other.

"Kiddlings?" I almost laughed, but of course, I didn't. During the time the two were peering into the darkness, I barely breathed.

"They wouldn't have come into the dark," the other said. "These sentients prefer light. They always head for the light."

The men stood there a moment in the doorway, took one final look around, then closed the door quietly, as if they didn't want anyone to hear.

Clara and I stayed in our hiding spots for a good five minutes before she began cranking up the light again. I wheeled my chair to face her, constantly glancing back at the door.

I took note that Dad's office was filled with things we could use as a weapon, if necessary, but how could you fight policemen – even if you were sure that's not who they were? Besides, our parents were back in the house. We didn't want to do anything that would put them in any more danger.

Still, I picked up a couple of hoof picks. They were nasty weapons if you used as one. Each had a hook at the end, one that wasn't super sharp but was very, very sturdy. Clara had the pots, which I realized she planned to use as weapons. Smart girl.

I am sure my parents would have wanted us to stay in the garage, but we couldn't hear anything from there. For all we knew, everyone was gone, and we were all alone, shivering in an unheated garage. Yes, we could have turned on the heater. Dad kept an electric one right next to his desk, but it was noisy. We didn't dare.

Clara dragged a couple of horse blankets over. Full of horsehair and smelling like horse, they weren't the nicest things to have over our bodies, but they were better than turning into popsicles.

I figured we'd been out in the office for at least thirty minutes. It was time to get closer to the action. Still wearing our twin red plaid horse blankets, Clara opened the door, and we slipped inside the house, back into the kitchen where a wild swath of pots and pans now lay across the floor. Apparently, the policemen had cleared out the cupboards. Had they thought we were hiding there? Although Clara was a lot smaller than I was, even she couldn't fit inside those narrow shelves. Weird.

The house was quiet. We couldn't hear either voices or footsteps. Had everyone left? Had they gone down to the basement or gone back where they came from? In that case, where were Mom and Dad?

I closed my eyes to hear better. I opened them again when I heard Clara making her way across the wooden floor of the kitchen. She was edging toward the doorway into the dining room. I bit my tongue to keep from calling out. I didn't need to worry. Clara whirled around and, with eyes as big and round as half dollars, whispered, "Slurpinthal is still there, still under the table!"

That was a surprise. My hands pushed my wheelchair closer to the doorway. I had to see. Apparently, Slurpinthal heard us coming. His eyes followed our progress, then he bolted, running into the kitchen to join us.

"They gone. Took Mother parent and father parent. Now all gone."

The house was empty? Clara and I looked at each other. Why was Slurpinthal still whispering then? Why had he remained in hiding under the table?

As if he felt our questions, he shook his head, patted his cheek with his pointer finger, and said, "Sh. They hear. They come."

"Where are they?" I asked, mouthing the words without any sound.

Clara started to cry. I grabbed at her hand and pulled her closer.

"Sh," I said.

She nodded, but her tears continued to fall. "Mom. Dad," she mouthed, moving her lips but making no noise.

Slurpinthal reached out to touch her cheek. He wiped his finger across her face, as if puzzling over my sister's tears.

"We cannot go to my house," he told us without moving his lips or speaking a sound.

My mouth shot open. Clara's tears stopped as she stared. She had heard him, too. Was he speaking into our minds?

"Who are you?" Clara asked, whispering.

You know. You both know. I do not come to hurt you. I do not come to do bad. I am here to help. Only to help.

He seemed to speak more clearly when he didn't talk out loud. I almost mentioned that, but then I remembered the situation with our parents. The important thing was to find them and to get them back. All the other questions didn't matter right now.

As if Slurpinthal read that, he nodded. *Good. We will hunt for them. We will use my newest tool.*

Clara released my hand and walked over to the refrigerator. She opened it, peered inside and reached for three bottles of water. She handed one to me, one to Slurpinthal, and then shoved one into the backpack of my wheelchair. Next, she handed me the horse blanket she'd been wearing, motioned that she was going up to her room, and took off in a gallop.

Slurpinthal drank his water. I reached back and slid the bottle she'd handed me into the backpack with hers. Then I made sure the backpack was properly closed. We might need the water later, but right then, all I wanted to do was to find my parents.

"Where is this tool of yours?" I asked Slurpinthal, trying to use my mind to ask the question.

He pointed outside. I turned to look and noticed that the weather was milder than before. It was still raining, but gently. The wind had died down. The trees were no longer dancing, but hanging low, like they'd released all their energy and were tired from their earlier boogie. The trees were probably waterlogged as well. I wondered if it would be possible to propel my wheelchair forward. If the ground were too muddy, I'd get stuck.

No problem, Slurpinthal said, grinning. He touched one wheel, bent over my lap, and placed his hand on the other. *Simply think where you want to go. It will take you now.*

I wrinkled my forehead and concentrated on being transported to my parents, but the chair didn't move. Slurpinthal shook his head sadly. *No, it is not a magic chair. It merely conducts a focus.*

I had no idea what that meant. I sighed and pushed with my hands. Slurpinthal stood beside me, looking down, tilting his head as if he could not understand why the chair wasn't moving in the manner he thought it should.

When Clara returned, she was wearing a heavy pink sweatshirt, the jeans she'd had on before, plus her pink polka dot raincoat with her new matching rainboots. She tossed me my comfortable old, gray sweatshirt and the new raincoat Mom had bought me.

I had known that my sister was smart, but this was far beyond what a five-year old should have figured out was needed. But that wasn't all. She also had brought my old coat for Slurpinthal. She handed it to him. It was the one that some of Dad's cow medicine had stained with patches of luminescent green, but it would work for a stormy night.

"Good work," I mouthed and gave Clara a thumbs-up signal.

Earlier, I'd thought the house felt cold, but then the horse blankets had kept me warm, and later the sweatshirt and coat Clara had brought me, but I hadn't realized that the chill was coming from the open front door. As we walked forward, me pushing the wheels as usual despite Slurpinthal's hocus pocus, we discovered that water was puddling on the wooden floor of the entryway. Mom would be very upset. In fact, she'd be furious because wood didn't like having a swimming pool on top of it. That warped the wood and took off its shiny finish.

For a moment I thought about turning back for a towel to clean up the mess, but there were sometimes when you just couldn't deal with normal problems. You had to ignore them and go beyond — straight into the weird. That's what we were doing, I decided, as I shut the door behind us.

While Slurpinthal and I were waiting for Clara, I'd picked up the flashlight from Mom's tool drawer. I turned it on now and set it on my lap. The light made me feel brave. I sort of felt like I'd picked up a device for magical protection. From the cold outside and from my fear, I was still shivering and wishing that a flashlight really could be magical.

Of course, I knew that idea was silly, but sometimes having a thought can give you almost the same reaction as if it *were* real. The flashlight was hard. It felt heavy in my lap. It felt like having it was a good thing, something that might be essential. Besides, its light was useful.

Clara had a flashlight, too, but hers was smaller and she had to keep winding it. That made its light flicker and wane. Because mine was new and large, with fresh batteries, the intensity of it made everyone cluster around me. Or maybe it was because we were all wet and cold — and scared.

We walked down the ramp at the entrance to our house. I could hear Slurpinthal and Clara stepping over puddles by the unevenness of their tread. Of course, I pushed right through the water. It splashed me. My feet grew cold, and my hands got wet and roughened by the chaff of the water on the rubber wheels. I wished I'd brought my gloves. Where were they? Why hadn't I remembered to get them?

Chapter Nine:
A Shed the Size of
a Football Field

The current shower was a steady drizzle that slid down the back of my neck, falling into whatever warmth my body's jacket once supplied. Yet, with a real, live alien beside us and my little sister, I couldn't whine about it, so I kept going, pushing my wheels forward into the hopeless river of our driveway, splashing and sloshing as rain steadily bombarded its endless streams of misery.

My nose was running. I couldn't wipe it, not while I was pushing myself forward. I stopped several times and did a quick swipe with the back of my hand, but we hadn't gone much farther than the distance to our van when Slurpinthal stopped and shook his head at me.

Think the direction, he ordered.

Slurpinthal had somehow moved to stand in front of me. His beady eyes stared down into mine. His face was eerie with the darkness of the night, but, maybe because of the flashlight, he appeared to glow even more strangely.

I sputtered, muttering to myself about people who believed in magic. Slurpinthal only shook his head again, and then shouted into my head, *I push, then*.

He didn't give me the opportunity to argue. Almost in the blink of an eyelash, he had jumped behind me. I was uneasy about having an alien at my back, but I'd lost all control over sanity a long time ago. I was in alien waters, so to speak. I shrugged, pulled my raincoat hood closer about my neck, and let Slurpinthal steer and push the wheelchair.

He must have been stronger than he looked. The wheelchair flowed smoothly. I let my hands on the armrests relax a bit. I'd been clutching them tightly, fearing that the alien might spill me down into the mud.

We walked for several minutes, Slurpinthal behind me, Clara beside me. Then, without feeling anything different, I realized that Slurpinthal was on the other side of me, striding along in the muddy water as if he'd forgotten he was supposed to be pushing.

Only, my chair was still going forward, smooth and easy as if it were on ice, skidding down an easy-flowing hill. But we weren't going downhill. In fact, there was a gentle incline. My chair should not be moving forward!

"What's going on?" I cried out, but Slurpinthal's finger was quickly on my cheek.

Do not talk. I feel them. They are near.

Meanwhile, the wheelchair rolled on, soundless, and without effort. It was then that I understood more clearly the ramifications of the night: Clara and I were in way over our heads. Things were getting stranger and stranger. I was too tired to argue about it, though. I leaned back against my seat and let the strangeness flow about me.

Although the sky seemed a bit lighter now that the dark rain clouds were passing, it was still a night with no stars or moon. Darkness feeds fear, I guess, for with the difficulty of pushing my wheelchair being taken care of by some magical force, my mind was free to dwell on the spookiness of the hour.

Outside the field of the flashlight I held, there were aliens, aliens who had kidnapped my parents, but I couldn't think of that. Instead, my mind dwelt on horror film kinds of things, like zombies walking at midnight or werewolves prowling the suburbs.

It seemed like I was hearing an abundance of night noises: owls whistling and hissing, rustles where nothing was visible, and small rodent things scurrying and darting about. Just animals, I supposed, although what creatures would bother to walk about on a rainy, cold night?

The trees had taken on a spookiness they didn't normally have. Their branches looked like monster fingers. Their bark held dark images, twisted into grimaces of evil. Even the gravel we walked on clattered with a hollow sound that was just plain creepy. I suppose it was only because the surface we were walking on was wet, yet the sound echoed. It was as if behind us there were more wheelchaired boys and a girl plodding along in rubber boots. I thought I heard the rattle of chains, too. I started to mention that, but I couldn't speak.

Something oohed from a circle of bushes. I stared but saw nothing. I was positive it was a ghost. With wide eyes, I kept looking, searching for it, wondering when it was going to jump out and say, "Boo." But it didn't. We continued on.

The cold dampness of the air had felt at first like a slap on the face, but as we made our way forward, I noticed my cheeks were turning numb. A deep burning sensation on my nose and lips felt like they were being bathed in acid.

We walked/wheelchaired for hours. Maybe it just seemed like that. I don't remember, but I do know we ended up at a small shed about a mile from Slurpinthal's house. I'd never seen it before, yet I'd explored the entire neighborhood before my accident. The shed must be new.

Slurpinthal didn't use a key to unlock it. He simply walked inside. Clara and I exchanged glances. Then we shrugged. She headed inside. Unfortunately for me, the door was too small for entry. When I tried to go forward, my chair got stuck. I could see from the width of my chair that I wasn't going to fit.

Slurpinthal suddenly did something to the door which enabled me to slide right in. Only he hadn't touched the entrance. He hadn't even been near it.

Did my chair get smaller, or did the door widen? I didn't ask. Clara was right. All we could do was accept the weirdness.

Inside, the shed was at least twice as big as it had appeared from the outside, and Slurpinthal waved us toward the back where a long staircase led downwards. I stared at it and backed away. "I can't go down there," I told him.

Your mind will take you, he said, and then, pushing from behind, he sent me forward and down.

I didn't scream. I just clung to the armrests and prayed that I'd survive the fall. When you can't walk, when your legs are useless, plummeting downwards is even more fearful than it would be for someone else. You see, I'm getting stronger with my therapy, but I still can't fall out of the wheelchair and pull myself back in. When I reached the ground, if I survived the fall, I'd be stuck on the ground, unmoving.

Needless to say, there was also the pain of the fall, and the thought that this time I might paralyze the rest of me. Any kind of tumble took me back to when the accident happened — the jolt, the crack, the void in time, the heavy blackness of unconsciousness.

It took perhaps twenty seconds before I realized my chair wasn't tilting forward. I wasn't doing a nose-dive, nor was I crashing, plummeting or diving down into the basement below. I was merely following the stairs in an escalator-like downward motion.

When I reached the floor, there was no impact. I just slid forward smoothly into a space even bigger than that above and then I stopped. The basement of this shed, where no shack used to be, was a room as big as a skating rink or maybe even larger — an airplane hangar.

Clara, her face turned to watch, her mouth open, her eyes filled with tears, ran to me and threw her arms around my neck. "You're okay," she said. "I thought . . ."

When she pulled away, we stared at each other. Her face was splotched with tears. I think mine must have looked the same, for I discovered that I, too, had been crying.

Over here, our alien buddy called out. Clara was the first to look away. She wiped her eyes with the sleeve of her sweatshirt, then turned back to catch hold of the handle bars of my wheelchair.

"I know you can make it go," she said, "but I want to push. I want to do something normal. You know what I mean?"

I nodded. Like Clara, I craved normality. The size of the room, the way it looked — shiny gray, shimmery even, was pretty off-setting. It was like entering a tree house and finding yourself in a palace with elegant mirrors and Oriental carpets. Nothing fit. Nothing seemed right.

As Clara pushed me forward toward Slurpinthal, my eyes tried to take it all in. As I'd said, the walls reflected, not us, exactly, although if you looked really hard, you could see yourself. But when I didn't concentrate on seeing myself, when the wall didn't mirror back at me, there were other images, shifting images, like a movie out of focus. The ceiling was like that too, except you couldn't stare at it very long. It made you dizzy.

Slurpinthal was standing beside a huge machine. How I knew it was a machine, I couldn't say. I suppose, it was because *the whatever it was* looked boxy, but the corners were rounded with all the angles smoothed out.

There were circles of light that rippled outward. Each light had its own color, vivid with intensity in the centers and as they revolved, lighter until all the beams faded into shimmers of silvery streaks that seemed threadlike, wavering in an unseen and unfelt breeze.

Slurpinthal didn't have to tell us not to touch anything. We wouldn't have. In fact, as Clara pushed me forward, I wanted to scream out, "Stop. Don't go forward."

But Slurpinthal was still waving us closer. He wanted us beside him, beside that frightening machine.

Look into it, he ordered. *Peer down and find them, find the ones you have lost.*

With that invitation, Clara and I did move forward. "This is a people finder, then?" I asked, feeling like an idiot.

Slurpinthal stared at me a moment. His eyes looked like orange peel rind, like the carrots he'd earlier eaten. I wondered about that. I wondered about a lot of things. But first things first. I looked down into the circles and thought about my parents.

It will find them. Yes. It will do that and more.

Clara hung back. She was gripping my wheelchair. I could feel her breathing down my neck.

"Do you smell that?" she asked. "Do you?"

That made me glance back at her. Clara often became intensely aware of odors the moment before she "saw" something. I wished I could see her face now, look into her eyes, but I couldn't turn that way. My body didn't allow that kind of mobility.

"Slurpinthal," I called out. "Watch my sister. She's about to see the future."

I'd never told anyone that. It was our family's secret, but things were weird, and Slurpinthal was special. I guess that's why I blurted it out like that.

Anyway, it made him look at her, just as she cried out and collapsed. I don't know how he caught her. It was impossible from the distance he'd stood, yet he did. He kept her from knocking her head on that funny machine of his.

"Where should I put her?" Slurpinthal asked. "Will she empty herself as your mother did?"

I shook my head. Clara didn't vomit after her sight. She merely fluttered her eyes a moment and sat up. Then, sometimes, she spoke of what she'd seen. Sometimes, she just stared at us as if wondering who we were. This time was one of the latter.

"Why. Who?" she said when her eyes opened.

I pushed forward. "Are you okay?" I asked, not that I had any doubts, but because I wanted her to see that I was there, and she wasn't alone with some strange alien neighbor that we hardly knew.

The moment Clara saw me, she relaxed. "I saw them. They were tied up. It was dark. Damp. I heard water dripping. Dad was talking. They hadn't put a – a gag in his mouth. Mom's head was tilted to the side. I think she was sleeping, but then who was Daddy talking to? No one else was there. They were alone."

"That is good," Slurpinthal interrupted. "Where are they?"

"I thought your machine was going to tell us that," I snapped, angry that he'd broken into Clara's speech. She needed time to tell her recollections. But, she also needed to relate it while it was fresh in her mind.

Clara blinked. Her eyes widened as she stared at Slurpinthal. "You were there," she said. "I saw you. You were outside — at the window, peering down at them. Daddy was talking to you."

How could this be? I am here. Slurpinthal thought at her and at me. His eyebrows were pushed up, sticking to his hair as if his eyebrows had come unfastened. He looked puzzled. His eyes were slanted and smaller than before. They looked less orange, too.

He didn't understand that Clara was seeing into the future. I opened my mouth to explain, but I didn't know how to explain that. No one else believed in clairvoyance. Not even my parents — well, not exactly. And why had Clara mentioned seeing only Slurpinthal in her dream? Where had she and I been? Hadn't we gone to save our parents?

As I was debating with myself how much, what, and why, Clara turned her gaze from my face back to Slurpinthal's. "You must go," she said. "They need you."

Slurpinthal had been staring at me, waiting for me to explain. Now he transferred his gaze down to my five-year-old sister. The orange of his eyes paled. The pupils grew larger. *You know where they are,* he asked. *How can I get to them?*

Clara shook her head. "I saw them, but I don't know where they are. It's not like that. I see pictures. I feel their fear and their hope when they see you."

I used the strength of my hands and arms to lift myself higher in the chair. Sometimes, if I wasn't careful, I started to slide down. Slurpinthal's eyes went to me. *Help her to recall.*

Of course. I nodded. "Clara, describe what you saw. Did you smell anything?"

She smiled at me with a quick flash of teeth, like things were normal. "How did you know? It was stinky. It smelled like, well like that time Mom forgot to take the clothes out of washing machine. Remember? The clothes were nasty. They were still a little wet, but they had black spots on them — mildew, Mom called it. Remember how she had to throw everything away? She put it into a plastic bag and tied it. But it still stank. That's what it smelled like where Mom and Dad were."

I took a long breath, expelled it slowly. That didn't sound good. A place that smelled of mildewing laundry wasn't a good place to be.

"That's good, Clara. That gives us lots of clues," I said, although I still had no idea where they could be." I thought for a moment. "Did you hear anything? Were there waves in background?"

She laughed. "No, no waves. They weren't by the ocean, Kyle. But there was water. It was dripping. And something more."

She paused and put her finger on her top lip. She tapped it several times. It was a gesture that Mom always did. I wondered if Clara was copying it, or if she'd just inherited the habit.

"I know. What I heard was like the sound of the vet case being jiggled up and down. You know, like things hitting things. I mean metal things. Bridle bits. Spurs…"

"Spoons and forks?" I asked, mentally jumping up and down because we'd found a second clue.

"So, could it be a restaurant?" I asked, watching Clara's face to see if she nodded.

This future you see, Slurpinthal interrupted. *You see me, but why? Why am I there and not here with you?*

101

I'd been so busy probing Clara, I hadn't noticed that Slurpinthal had moved back to his machine. He looked like he was adjusting something, his fingers moving a dial that clicked softly each time he touched it. I started to ask him what he was doing, but the machine gave a loud burp, and Slurpinthal nodded.

It has found them, he said. *They are in my basement lab.*

It was too easy. I wanted to argue. I wanted to prod Clara more, searching for clues. Yet, if Slurpinthal had found them, I didn't want to waste more time. "Are you sure? Is that machine reliable?"

"Yes," Clara said. "I remember now. They were looking up through a window with bars. I think it was your basement window. Kyle and I used to look inside — before you came, I mean," she added, looking up at Slurpinthal shyly.

Then, I know what the clink of metal was — they must be trying to figure out my research.

Slurpinthal's ears had begun to flap slightly. I thought at first that it was my imagination, but it wasn't. I noticed Clara staring at the ears, too. She smothered a giggle and then looked away.

I still wasn't convinced the machine had found my parents. "What about the mildew thing. If that's your lab, do you have wet clothing growing black spots hanging around as decoration?"

The moment the words left my mouth, I realized I sounded sarcastic. Dad would have given me an *attitude adjustment,* as he called it. Mom would have asked me to spend some time alone in my room, recalling how polite people communicated.

Slurpinthal didn't even wiggle a whisker — where had that expression come from? But as I stared, Slurpinthal's face took on new growth — real cat whiskers that first sprouted, then began growing long and straight.

Clara started giggling, pointed at the whiskers, and said, "You look like a kitty cat. I'm so glad. I like cats. Will you grow fur, too?"

Slurpinthal's eyes flitted from me to my sister. Then he smiled. *They are merely air particle analyzers. I have grown them to improve our odds.*

Most of the time, Slurpinthal was only a little strange, but this new ability was beyond strange. It was abnormal. It was ALIEN. To be able to grow something just because you wanted to. . . No one on Earth could do that — no one human, and that was a fact.

I took a long, deep breath, but not because I was preparing to say something. What was there to say? I just needed a long, deep breath. I mean, wouldn't you if your parents had been kidnapped, you were in a shack that had suddenly turned into a football field full of machines and shiny surfaces, and now, you found yourself sitting next to a creature who spoke into your mind and sprouted whiskers?

Slurpinthal eyed me. His head tilted. His ears stilled. His nose twitched. (Yes, really. Another adaptation, I figured. Was this like the wolf telling Little Red Riding Hood that he'd grown parts of his face to better see, smell, and taste her?)

I do not hang clothes in my basement lab. I grow mushrooms on one side. I believe that is the smell Clara recalls from her dream. I have a variety of mushrooms, some that smell like garlic, others that have the odor of cabbage. That's the one that Clara probably smelled.

She should be glad that I got rid of the most putrid ones. The Stinkhorn and the Northern Tooth Mushrooms both have an odor of rotten meat. My favorite, however, are the Amanita's. I like their smell. They smell like raw potatoes.

I nodded. "Could we go save my parents now?"

Slurpinthal shook his head. *The younger one is too fatigued. We must sleep. We need to regain energy. We will need to be fully restored tomorrow when we go to save your father/mother. But now, we must rest.*

I can't tell you exactly what it was that we slept on. Slurpinthal walked over to the side of the room, pressed a red spot on the wall three times, and suddenly, there were holes forming in what had been a vertical, flat surface. The spaces squeezed inward and hollowed out.

I thought, at first, that they were cupboards where he kept things like books or maybe even food, but as the openings elongated and deepened, I began to understand their purpose. Clara hopped right into the smallest one and lay down. She looked comfortable, and I could see from her breathing that she'd fallen asleep almost the moment she put her head down on the attached white cushion.

I wasn't as sure about trusting Slurpinthal. I think he saw that, for he inserted himself into a second chamber, and then, just like Clara, he immediately closed his eyes, and his chest began a slower movement up and down, up and down.

I stood watching him, studying him to see if his sleep was real, but how could I tell? How did an alien sleep? While watching his room all those nights, I'd never seen the lights go out. I hadn't known he ever slept.

The room, which had been light a moment before, began to gray. It was getting dark inside. I switched my flashlight back on and directed the light about the room. The walls that had a moment before been white were turning black. The glow at the top of each panel was dimming. In a moment, my flashlight would be almost the only light in the basement.

The machine that Slurpinthal had been so intent on using had even stopped gurgling. Its light had paled, but it hadn't gone out. Maybe the computer in it was still probing something. I started to move closer, hoping it would show me something, but a sudden yawn pierced my thoughts. My head felt heavy. My arms were practically hanging with weariness. I could barely keep my eyes open.

Giving in to what the alien apparently wanted me to do, I wheeled myself over to the remaining wall opening. Using what was left of the strength in my arms, I pulled my tired body into the gap, tugged at my legs until they were in the correct position, and then lay back. Immediately and without dreams, I slept.

Chapter Ten:

Let's Go Save Our Parents

In the morning, I woke to find Clara grabbing at my shirt. I think she was frightened that I had died or something because once again her eyes were teary.

"Okay. I'm awake," I said, and she stopped pulling at me and smiled.

"Slurpinthal is getting us something to eat," she told me, as I swung my legs to the side and down, then worked at getting myself back into the chair.

Food was a good thing, but more urgent was the necessity of changing my urine sack. I didn't want to leak all over Slurpinthal's lab.

"Is there a bathroom?" I asked.

Clara nodded and pointed it out, then stepped aside so I could wheel my way toward it.

Doing a urine dump is something I perform at least twice a day. I have to detach the plastic bag attached to my belt and pour out the collected liquid. It no longer even takes thought. I washed up, dabbed my face with water, and went in search of Slurpinthal and the food he was offering.

I was pleasantly surprised with the granola bars and pouches of orange juice he gave us. I'd been half-expecting to be given mushrooms, green leaves, or carrots, the only foods I'd seen him eat.

After breakfast, we returned to stand in front of the machine and peer down inside it. The machine confirmed that our parents were still in Slurpinthal's basement. Clara seemed cheered by that. I think because of her premonition, she'd decided the problem had already been solved. She hadn't stopped to think that she'd only seen our parents behind the bars of Slurpinthal's window. Her vision didn't show them freed.

While we were staring at the machine, I noticed Slurpinthal's whiskers were vibrating slightly as if he was using them to gather more information. At least, that's what I suspected because once more, he looked like a cat when it sniffs something interesting.

I was grateful Slurpinthal's whiskers could help us free our parents, but I wondered about how sensitive they were. What exactly could they pick up? Shouldn't there be a law against whiskers that could read things people might not want them to read? Of course, maybe Slurpinthal could do that with or without the whiskers.

Despite what my sister had said the day before about only Slurpinthal being in the image of her premonition, both Clara and I wanted to go rescue our parents. I suggested, at first, that Clara should stay behind. Slurpinthal said that only he should go. Both Slurpinthal and my sister kind of hinted that it would be better if I were not involved, but I had no intention of remaining.

Imagine my parents being rescued by my five-year-old sister, alone with an alien, and me, nowhere nearby. We argued about it all through the granola bars. While Slurpinthal munched and Clara drank, I made it clear that I wouldn't stay behind. Clara did the same. And of course, no one suggested that Slurpinthal remain behind. So, it was finally agreed that we would all go.

Unfortunately, that decision brought me smack against the next obstacle. How was I going to get up out of the basement? I asked Slurpinthal about an elevator.

He shook his head. *The chair will take you up,* he told me.

That didn't sound like a good idea at all, but what could I do? I wasn't sure that I could crawl up the steps. It was a long way to the top. Besides, even if I could make it to the top, I'd need the chair once we got there in order to continue on our way.

I suggested that maybe Slurpinthal could carry the wheelchair, but he shook his head.

The chair will take you up, he repeated.

So we set out, Slurpinthal walking behind me. He placed his hands on the handles and pushed my wheelchair, his small body applying no more force than Clara always did. I didn't need him to drive me forward. My hands were quite capable of that, but I didn't argue about it. I was still stewing over getting up the stairs.

When I felt the first stair against the wheel of my chair, I came back to awareness and cried out, "You can't push me up the stairs!"

As if he hadn't heard me, Slurpinthal continued to push me against the staircase. That could cause only one thing to happen. I was going to tip over. My mouth opened to tell him so when the chair began to lift. It didn't raise me up very high. It wasn't as if I were suddenly in an elevator. It was only that instead of bumping up on to the step, I flew slightly above it. That motion continued as the chair mimicked someone climbing steep stairs.

When I reached the top, Clara was already there. Without a word, she took over, wheeling me away from the opening, pushing me to the side. We waited until Slurpinthal was on the same level as us, then,

Clara, getting behind me again, pushed me forward across the flooring and out the door.

The ground was slighter drier that morning, but it was still rough going. When Clara began to pant, I closed my eyes and imagined the wheelchair going forward, and it did. My poor sister let go and walked beside me, her hand on my shoulder.

"That's really cool," she said, whispering and bending over so she could speak into my ear. "Do you think you could do that if Slurpinthal wasn't behind us?"

That was something I'd been wondering, too, but I didn't respond. I was busy thinking about what we were about to do and questioning why none of us had thought to call the police. Shouldn't we have already done so? Was it too late to call them?

I blinked, stopped my forward movement, and turned to face Slurpinthal. "We need to. . ." I said, but something in the way Slurpinthal looked at me reminded me that we weren't supposed to talk out loud.

Apparently my squelched sentence didn't matter. My thoughts must have transferred just as easily without finishing the sentence, for Slurpinthal began to shake his head. His eyes sagged. Even his whiskers drooped.

The police cannot help. If they were called, they would not believe. If they did come, they would only be in the way. Those who have taken your parents are not from your world. They might harm those who tried to shoot them. They would certainly not surrender those captured. Your officials would not frighten them.

I suppose I should have figured that out. But we were always told to call 911 when something bad happened. Even at school, everyone said to trust the police to solve all our problems. Didn't they have experience dealing with everything — even aliens? Would the police really not be able to help?

Clara was watching me. Her eyes grew large and frightened. She was shivering a bit, too, as if the cold and all the horror that had been happening to us was suddenly penetrating through her sweatshirt and coat.

My sister was only five, I reminded myself. Of course she was starting to wear down. "Come sit with me," I said, wishing I could move over to let her sit beside me, but I couldn't do that, not even with the help of Slurpinthal. My lower body was a lump that didn't move.

Clara eyed me, tilting her head in a way that reminded me of our alien friend. Had Clara begun to copy him?

She took a step forward, then hesitated. I reached out for her shiny raincoat, grabbed at it, and pulled her backwards and down into my lap.

"There," I said. "Just rest a minute. The wheelchair is no more difficult to move with your weight than without. This power Slurpinthal has given me doesn't seem to care." As I said that, I started us forward, slowly at first, as if checking that I could indeed do what I'd said.

My sister was stiff for a while as if she thought she might be too much of a burden, but after a moment or two, I felt her relax.

The clouds had been swept away during the night. The sky had awakened to the blue of lake water. The air, although not warm, was warmer than the night before. It wasn't unpleasant to be rolling along the road toward our cul-de-sac.

Even the birds seemed friendly that morning. They trilled, cooed, and chirped as most contented, feathered creatures seemed to do. As we progressed, Clara pointed out a quail with babies. We both giggled as a blue jay screeched its irritation at our presence in his territory.

Your world is kind in the morning, Slurpinthal said into our minds. *In my world, there are no flying things, no morning songs, no cheery sky of red and gold. I like your world, and I like you humans very much.*

Clara turned to look at me. I think we made a face at each other. I didn't know if Slurpinthal could read our minds at that moment, but we were both thinking about how unfriendly Slurpinthal had been the first time we'd met him. He hadn't seemed as if he liked humans then. He'd acted like my family and I were only slightly safer than a dog with rabies.

When we arrived at the house where Slurpinthal currently lived, we took note that there were no lights visible through any of the windows. Of course, the sun was fully up. It was possible the aliens didn't need more light. Clara said that maybe only the lights down in the basement were on.

As we slipped into the backyard, we discovered she was right. A yellow glow lit up the room down beneath the ground like phosphorous lights up a cave. Someone was down there all right. Was it our parents?

Without a word to us, Slurpinthal crept forward. He could be very quiet when he wanted. His shoes, although they looked normal enough, must have been special ones, because they didn't creak or squeak. Slurpinthal was as quiet as a Native American in moccasins, at least the Hollywood ones on TV.

I wanted to join him, to be part of the excitement, so to speak, but I knew my chair would displace gravel and make more noise than a pack of wolves. I sighed and sat still.

I thought Clara looked like she was itching to go forward, too, but after a moment, she turned to look at me and said, "This is what I saw, Kyle. It's what I saw yesterday. Slurpinthal will be looking down at them, and they will talk to him. Now what comes next? Why couldn't I see farther?"

Her face was all twisted with worry, her eyes slanted, her forehead wrinkled. She looked like a wizened old woman. I sighed and patted her arm.

This kind of thing always bothered Clara. She could get an image of the future, but nothing that she could pick and choose. She couldn't say, "I want to see what happens to so and so after the awful thing I just saw." She couldn't force herself to see beyond a premonition. She could only see the moment revealed to her by this strange power she had.

Sometimes I thought that a fractional piece of the future might be even worse than not knowing what was going to happen in the whole event. One little mysterious peek was almost a tease. It must really be frustrating.

Still, she was super young. Was it possible she could gain more ability later? Did people with ESP widen their range with age? It was something I decided to look up when I went to the library the next time. I mean, maybe there were exercises she could do. Maybe she needed to take more vitamins or use herbs to increase her brain power. Would a library book give that kind of information?

I didn't speak of it, however. My eyes were on Slurpinthal as he crept forward into the bushes that surrounded his basement window. We saw him kneel. Then we couldn't see him at all. He was shorter than the bush he'd crept behind, plus he kind of blended in with the leaves around it. In fact, as I thought about it, maybe he was like an octopus, able to change colors to match his surroundings. There was a lizard that did that, too, but I couldn't think of its name at the moment.

Clara's finger, not her thumb, but her index, made its way into her mouth. She sucked on it sometimes when she was the most worried. Mom would get after her if she caught her doing that. Mom would say something like, "Don't you dare wreck your teeth, Clara. We can't afford braces. Besides, fingers are full of germs."

I wish I could hear Mom speaking right now, even if she was lecturing. I wish she were here with us. I closed my eyes and prayed that she soon would be.

The early morning was growing warmer. I took off my raincoat and unzipped my sweatshirt. Clara eyed me and then took off hers.

She stood up and came over to whisper into my ear. "I wish I had some cocoa."

I wasn't much of a cocoa fan. I liked chocolate, and I loved marshmallows —especially when roasted over an open fire — but cocoa? It didn't do a thing for me. I'd rather drink some milky coffee. I liked to pour half a cup, dump in some sugar, and then fill it up to the rim with milk. That was the good stuff.

Mom and Dad didn't let me have it very often. They said they weren't sure it was good for me, but I sneaked it pretty regularly. They always had a pot of coffee on, and they didn't notice when a little of it disappeared. A cup of Joe, as Dad called it, would taste really good right now.

Over to the right, I saw Kevin Buell tossing papers from his bike. He was old enough to have a paper route. I'd asked him about it, interviewing him for a project we had to do. He'd been okay about talking to a kid my age. In fact, he'd been really nice.

The town paper, "The Sun Valley Tin Can Kicker," wasn't a very exciting paper to work for, Kevin had explained. It didn't have a lot of important stuff, he'd told me —just local things, like who'd just had a baby and who was getting married or had died. There were party announcements and store sales. Lots of advertisements, he'd said, looking disgusted. He'd shown me all the ads for tires and women's dresses.

Kevin had red hair and freckles that dotted every inch of his face. He also had a smile full of what Dad called charisma. When Kevin smiled, everyone just had to smile back. He had that kind of personality, too. You wanted to be near him, to hear what he had to say.

It was easy talking to him, although I hadn't said much. He'd done all the talking, as he eagerly showed me the want-ad section, which he said with a huge grin, had lots of dogs and cats being offered for absolutely nothing. I'd peered down at an ad for five puppies and wished, as always, that we could get an animal. (One that wasn't an alley cat, so we were actually allowed to touch it, hold it on our laps, and listen to it purr.)

That morning, Kevin didn't see us as we sat there on Mr. Slurpinthal's driveway. The teen was making a smooth loop, turning about because the Slurpinthal house was the last one on the cul-de-sac. I raised my hand to wave, just in case he turned and noticed us, but as Kevin's bike headed the opposite way, his eyes were on the houses he was passing. He never looked our way.

A pair of mourning doves were drinking from a puddle in the road. Their gray feathers were slicked back, their backs smooth and shiny. Clara's favorite bird was the blue jay. She liked the way it scolded everyone — and the prettiness of the males' feathers. I had to agree with her that blue jays were often the most beautiful of birds, but my favorite was still the mourning dove. I liked the sound of their coo and the fact that they mated for life. I wished humans did. I thought about that again, as I always did, worrying about my best friend and his divorcing parents.

The doves drank their fill and flew up into the peach tree. They bobbed their heads and stared at us, obviously wondering why we were in their yard.

When I looked at my sister, I saw that she was watching the birds, too.

"They won't get a divorce," she said. "They'll go away to a conference and come back different, nicer to each other. Then they'll be happier."

I knew that Clara was talking about Todd's parents. That made me smile and give a quiet little sigh. I wished I could tell Todd that and relieve him of his fear, but I couldn't ever tell what Clara had said. That was our family secret.

I would have asked Clara more about what she'd seen, but just at that moment, I heard the sound of a lawnmower, and I turned my wheelchair around and stared. It had sounded like the machine was about to mow Slurpinthal's grass, but it was only Mr. Clive giving his perfect lawn a manicure.

That's what Dad always called it. Dad only pretended to like the people he wasn't fond of. I wondered what Dad had against Mr. Clive. The man wasn't very friendly, but then, neither had Slurpinthal been the first day.

Clara suddenly pinched me. "I can't see Slurpinthal. Can you?"

I shook my head, patted her arm, and said, "He's there. I bet he's talking to Dad right now. Be patient." She nodded, sighed, and leaned back against me. I retreated back to my thoughts.

"What?" I demanded somewhat louder than I should have. I'd forgotten about the aliens for the moment. I don't think it mattered, though. Mr. Clive's mower was louder than a screaming monkey, which is what Mom often said.

Mom didn't like Mr. Clive because he mowed the lawn before the time it was allowed. According to the city ordinance, no power tools could be used before nine AM on Saturdays and Sundays, but despite complaints, Mr. Clive continued to cut his lawn at six thirty unless it was raining or he was out of town.

Since Mom was often groggy and mad because Mr. Clive had woken her up with his loud mower, Mom sometimes grumbled about certain people being inconsiderate, but Dad always took her in his arms and tickled her back into smiles.

Anyway, Mr. Clive continued to be Mr. Clive, which was rather rude and nasty. That was just the way he was. If a kid accidentally threw a ball in his yard, that kid never got the ball back. Mr. Clive kept it. A dog or cat that strayed into his yard got water sprayed or worse, and if someone rode their bike across his yard, you'd think it was fireworks time. Mr. Clive, even without his lawnmower, was LOUD.

Chapter Eleven:

My Idea

Clara was still clinging to me, but she suddenly socked my arm. "Wake up," she hissed. "He's coming out!" she said.

She didn't need to. I could see that Slurpinthal had stood up and was retracing his steps back to us. He was also alone — no parents in sight.

"Where are they?" I half-whispered, half-hissed when he was close enough to ask.

Clara shook her head. I glanced over and saw that her eyes were teary. I was suddenly no longer mad about the pinch or the arm slug. I pulled her toward me and gave her a quick hug. "They'll be okay. We'll save them, Clara."

Of course, a fool and his words are like water on an empty stomach. (No, that wasn't something I made up. I read it somewhere, and thought it was pretty good.) I wasn't saying that my words were foolish. I knew that we would save my parents. It's just that I didn't know exactly how.

Slurpinthal had made his way back to the driveway, doing that moccasin thing he did of walking without a sound. If I ever had time to ask all the questions I had, that would be one of them. How did he do that? He wasn't even wearing moccasins, but regular brown dress shoes, like my father wore when he wasn't wading through mud at one of the cow farms or horse ranches.

Parents are in the basement, for the moment. And treated well.

"Why didn't you get them out of there?" Clara whispered.

Slurpinthal shook his head. *Do not speak out loud. It is not safe here.*

He looked back at the house, his eyes studying what appeared to be a vacant house. Clara and I watched him, waiting. Neither of us could see anything to cause alarm. Probably the aliens were still asleep.

We will steal parents away tonight, Slurpinthal said. *I must get things. Blow window. Where do they sell such things?*

I shook my head and scratched something that itched on my arm. Wouldn't you know it, a spider had crawled up my wrist. It was only a dime-sized critter, but it still gave me the shivers. I hated spiders. It was lucky I didn't scream!

Come, we go back to other place.

"And leave Mom and Dad?

You must be quiet, he warned. *They hear.*

"So what. Let them. Let them try to capture us. I'll . . ."

Of course, that was all bluster. I had no weapons. I'd never learned karate or king fu, and even if I could actually move my legs anymore, I was just a kid, a sixth grader. We were supposed to rule the elementary school, but I wasn't one of those who could scare anybody. Besides I was stuck in a stupid wheelchair.

Clara threw herself across the space between us and landed with her arms around me. I wanted to throw her off, but I didn't. I was crying. Stupidly crying.

Clara didn't say anything. What was there to say? I'd been an idiot. Of course we must do what Slurpinthal said. What else could we do?

But then an idea bear conked me over the head, and I remembered Mr. Clive's lawnmower, still growling its way through the peace of the morning, chewing all the shaggy grass of his lawn. His lawnmower was a fantastic machine, the kind you could sit on, the kind that did everything you asked it to do as you simply sat and steered it around the yard.

Dad had once told me that Mr. Clive's lawnmower had a motor with more horse power than old Snowdrop. A Clydesdale would be able to pull window bars off the basement wall. And if that was so, couldn't Mr. Clive's lawnmower?

I gently pushed Clara away, motioned for Slurpinthal to come closer, and told him my idea.

Good, Slurpinthal said, nodding his head.

Clara began writhing her hands. They looked like dancing snakes. She was biting her lips, too. I knew she was going to argue. I watched as her lips burst open, and she protested, "But that's stealing. You can't take someone's mower without asking. Mom and Dad would never let us do that."

She had a point.

Slurpinthal eyed the two of us, looked back over his shoulder, and said, *We leave now. Come.*

I won't bore you with a description of our walk back to Slurpinthal's shed. Sure, I saw things like that black cat of the Peterson's, weaving his way in and out of the lanky reeds around the stream. The funny part about that is when the cat was hidden by the tall weeds, you could see this invisible tail striding along. It looked like a shark's fin standing up in the water or a cobra with its back to us. Except it bobbed and weaved in and out. The sight was so funny that Clara and I started giggling so hard we were in danger of falling out of my wheelchair. We might have, if I hadn't been holding on.

Slurpinthal merely tilted his head and looked at the tail. *Domestic cat,* he declared as if Clara and I didn't know that. He saw nothing strange or funny. I wondered if aliens had a sense of humor. Were they always serious?

As we continued to walk, I thought about that. Was it possible that humans were the only race that laughed just to be silly? Did aliens tell jokes? Did they have comics and funny movies? Did they do slapstick routines?

These were things I wanted to ask, but of course, we were still trying to be silent.

Slurpinthal sent another message into my brain: *Yes, we steal/borrow noisy machine. We break window. Save parents.*

Wasn't it weird that Slurpinthal could do that?. He seemed to react to things we thought as much as things we said. Didn't that get boring? How could he separate voices? Did Clara's voice sound different in mind speech than mine?

How did an alien weed out interesting voices from people he didn't want to hear? Like what if he heard Keven Buell's thoughts when the guy was tossing out a newspaper? Would that be confusing? And the cat? Did a cat send thoughts to an alien?

On the way to the shed, Clara and I saw a farmer plowing his field. That made me stop and watch, even though Slurpinthal kind of acted like we were in a hurry. But we weren't. He'd said we couldn't rescue my folks until nighttime, so what was the rush? I didn't say that, though. I just halted the chair for a moment and stared at the tractor.

You see, I've always thought that tractors were kind of cool. It was my secret ambition to get to try one out someday. Could a boy paralyzed from the waist down ever drive a tractor? I mean, I know there were ways around every complication. My physical therapist had shown me pictures of cars adapted for paraplegics. You could steer a car with your hands — or with your mouth even. You could power the gas pedal using only hands. "You can do all sorts of things with limited capacity for movement," the therapist told me so often I'd turned it into a chant so I could repeat it each session.

Limited capacity

Is not a limitation.

You can steer a car

With hands or

Attach it to your mouth.

You can always

Find an answer

It matters not the catch

For limited capacity

Is not a limitation.

I always did it like a rap song. Kind of nifty, huh? The therapist laughed the first time I sang it, but then the next time I came back, he wanted me to do it again and again. Then he made me speak into a microphone, and he recorded it.

He told me that he played it for all his clients. I wonder if I'd be sitting in the waiting room one day and hear someone rapping my song? That would be pretty incredible.

Maybe that meant I'd be famous someday, but I doubted it. I really couldn't sing. I just strung sounds together. That wasn't hard. Anyone could do that.

Anyway, before I came up with the chant, when the therapist just kept repeating his words about being able to do anything, he was encouraging me to work harder and strengthen the rest of my body. I started lifting weights to build my strength.

I can lift my whole body up. I can slide and manipulate my bones as if that half of me were nothing more than a sack of potatoes. I'm already pretty strong, too. But all that's just a temporary measure — for me.

That's why I don't have a motorized wheelchair, because soon I'm not going to need it. The doctor thinks he can get me walking again.

Mechanical adaptations are a good thing. I'm glad they're available, but I what I really wish for — no, what I pray for — is that the injections the doctor is giving me will stimulate my spinal cord enough that I can be normal again. Then I can drive a tractor or do anything else I want. That's the better plan. To be normal.

The sun was hot on my back. It was making the metal on my wheelchair uncomfortable, something I didn't want to touch. I guess that doesn't sound too important, but it is when you're stuck inside it. When the metal gets hot, any shift of my body means that the heated part burns. And if you've ever sat in a chair for very long, you know you have to keep shifting. Not to move your upper body enough so your lower body is budged a couple of inches, means you get sores on your bottom, and that's a really bad thing.

When we finally arrived at the shed, Slurpinthal did his unlock thing, and held the door wide for me to roll inside. Once inside, we were free to talk again, but then, inside that room, I didn't feel like talking. I started stewing about the stairs and how I was going to have to do that magic act of levitation. Whoops, that means rising up. What's the opposite of levitation? What do we call the horrid sensation of falling when you're not really falling — at least I hoped I wouldn't be.

Perhaps there wasn't a word for it, and I'd just have to invent one. *Downitation? Droppitation? Delevitation?* Or maybe, *Downleving?* The last was my favorite, so I decided to stick with it.

While I was musing over the precise word, Slurpinthal came up behind me. I didn't think of that. I kind of trusted him after all this time together. So I was peering downward and imagining what I was going to have to do, and I really, really didn't like the thought of what was about to come.

I started to back up and tell Clara and Slurpinthal that I'd decided to stay upstairs this time. I was just about to do so when my chair took off without my urging, levitated up, and hovered right in the middle of the long plunge downward.

I screamed out, "Stop it, Slurpinthal. Put me down!" but he didn't. I was flying, or at least doing a great imitation of a giant hummingbird sipping nectar.

If I'd been normal, I would have been kicking and screaming. As it was, I was just screaming loud enough to puncture eardrums. (Well, I've never actually seen that happen. I wouldn't really want to be the cause of someone's ear popping off like a busted balloon.)

Clara started crying. In fact, she was yanking on Slurpinthal's arm, trying to get him to do something. But he didn't move. He just stood there, staring at me, completely ignoring my sister. Oh, he knew she was having a tantrum, all right. He knew I was, too, but neither of those things made him budge. It was like he was frozen to the wooden floor, immobile as a statue.

Eventually, I stopped fighting the chair. My temper wasn't making anything move, and my throat hurt from the screams. I clamped my mouth shut, closed my eyes, and waited, hoping that something nice would happen — like Slurpinthal would do whatever magic it was that brought a floating wheelchair back down to terra firma.

A minute of that went by with Clara crying and me holding my eyes tighter than a tight-clenched fist, while Slurpinthal stood like a statue staring off into nothingland.

They say that time has no sound. But whoever said that was wrong. Time clicks and whirls and drips giant sweat drops sliming down your neck. Time is louder than a train thundering down the rail tracks, or it was for me in that frozen place of hovering.

Eventually, I opened my eyes. I opened them because Clara's crying had changed. It was like the sound of the thundering train I'd mentioned. I'd heard the noise of it many times — growing higher as it sped away. Clara's sound was like that. I opened my eyes to see why. Slurpinthal was dragging her toward the door, away from me.

Now, I'd said that I'd grown to trust the alien, but not if he were pushing me into a deep hole and carrying my sister away.

"Stop!" I called out. "Where are you taking her?"

Slurpinthal, hearing my voice, turned about. *You have endangered her. She attempted to rescue you. Although her bravery is praiseworthy, I cannot allow her to be harmed.*

"How could Clara possibly help me? I'm stuck in midair," I said, more puzzled than angry.

You are not stuck, only stubborn, and they are not the same at all.

Now that really made me angry. I was in danger of falling. My wheelchair was dangling over a chasm. How could Slurpinthal say that? How could he chuckle, as he was doing at that moment?

124

"Can you still move your chair?" my sister asked, sweeping her hair out of her eyes, and staring at me with red, swollen eyes, eyes that held dripping pools of tears.

Move the chair? Me? Ok, so I should have thought of that. I'd been directing the chair for the better part of two days. Yet, I hadn't thought of trying to order its direction. The idea hadn't occurred to me because I'd been certain that it was Slurpinthal who was controlling everything.

I took a deep breath. That's when it hit me. I'd panicked. I'd gotten scared and forgotten everything Slurpinthal had taught me. Not only that, but I'd also frightened poor Clara to tears.

"I can make it obey me, right, Slurpinthal?" I asked.

He smiled slightly, bobbed his head in imitation of our nods, and patted Clara on the head. *Do not worry, child. He understands now. He will do what is necessary.*

I felt like an idiot. It was so obvious once it bonked me on the head. Why hadn't I realized it? I connected my mind to the chair. . . Don't ask me how. It was just this thing I now knew how to do. I turned the on-switch, so to speak, and the chair lowered itself about an inch and continued following the steps downward.

When I was about halfway to the basement floor, the others slowly followed behind. It was such an easy process. The touchdown was hardly noticeable.

It was not because I was tired that my head sagged. I wanted to hide the redness of my face, but I shouldn't have bothered. Clara wasn't even aware of my shame. The moment she stepped on the basement floor, she ran straight to me, threw her arms around my neck, and wept in relief.

I took the wetness of her hug for about thirty seconds and then shrugged her off. "Clara, everything's fine," I said. "Don't cry anymore. Please."

Slurpinthal was watching this exchange. His eyes were orange-pupiled again. What did that mean? Why was I never able to read his facial changes?

As Clara moved away, he walked toward me. *You have mastered it. Now you understand.*

Understand? I'd never understand in a million years how I could mind-link with a wheel chair, but I didn't say anything, not about that. What I did say, in a rather mumbled undertone, is "I'm sorry, Slurpinthal, that I didn't trust you. I thought you were trying to kill me."

I might not be able to read his facial expressions well, but at that moment, I thought I could almost read his eyes. I think they showed a moment of extreme sadness, but it was only for a second, and then it was gone. Then he was moving away, telling us it was time to eat.

Chapter Twelve:

The Great Lawnmower Caper

We spent a long time in the underground basement — hours and hours. Slurpinthal said that we must all rest to be ready for what was to come, so we lay down in the little holes in the wall and slept. When we woke up, we ate again, and drew up our plans.

Clara didn't protest at all when they included *borrowing* the neighbor's lawnmower. She only wanted to know if Mom and Dad would be okay. Then when Slurpinthal continued to discuss the plan, my sister sat quietly, listening. Her upper lip trembled. I think her eyes dribbled a few drops of worry tears, but she kept quiet. I worried because she looked so pale.

When it was time, I went first. I engaged the will power switch on my brain/wheelchair connection and lifted myself up the stairs. It was easy that time. No hesitation. I arrived at the top, and the others followed.

The night was sultry. I was sweating before we'd gone a driveway's distance. I looked about at the others and saw that I wasn't alone. I wished we'd brought water bottles. I wished we could take a second shower. But I knew that Mom and Dad were waiting for us. I pushed on, as did the others.

The old owl was up in his tree again. He hissed at us from his well-hidden perch. Once that would have been frightening, but that night, the three of us only smiled at each other.

There was a moon that night. No clouds locked it in darkness. The moon gave us plenty of light to see our way. We didn't need the flashlights we'd brought just in case.

When we had gone about halfway, I saw that Clara was falling behind, her feet dragging, her head falling forward as if it were too heavy for her to hold up.

I motioned for her to come sit with me. She shook her head and walked on. She was a trooper. I was learning that about her. I watched as she jerked her head back up and strode forward, walking on stiff pride, if nothing else.

So we ambled on, each lost in our thoughts, silent as night animals fearing to be heard by a predator. And then Clara stumbled. This time, Slurpinthal swept her up in his arms and carried her to the chair.

"You must save your energy for the release of your parents. We will need you awake and ready then," he said.

Clara didn't argue. She wiggled into my lap, lay her head against my shoulder, and was asleep in seconds.

Slurpinthal and I moved forward, watchful-eyed and silent.

And then, our house came into sight. It looked deserted. Our car still stood in the driveway, the windows all tightly closed from the rain the night before.

The house was dark as if asleep, just as it would be if this were a normal night, and we were upstairs in our beds. Dad would be snoring. Mom would have a face free of makeup, her lips faded without the lipstick she usually wore. Clara would be in her room, the curtains in her window gently moving from the overhead fan.

And I would be in my bedroom with the Tyrannosaurus Rex stretching out its claws as if it could grab the moth fluttering about the window pane, captured by a single streak of moonlight.

What would we be doing in our adventures of the night? Silly dreams, things that couldn't happen — like nibbling on the fantasy world of wishes that included playing baseball, riding my bike, being popular at school, or maybe even something super outrageous like riding a dinosaur through the jungles of a prehistoric world, at least until Mom called out that it was time to get up. That was how it would be on a normal night if we were up in bed, asleep in our rooms. Oh, how I wish . . .

But instead, we were plugging along, out on the street, perspiration sticking to our bodies like frozen food left on the sink to thaw — dripping drops of sweat from the humidity of the air and from our fear.

Clara was sound asleep in my arms. She was making faint meowing sounds like she'd turned into a kitten. And there was an alien walking alongside my magical wheelchair.

We can't forget the alien because that's what the night was all about: the alien beside me, and the ones who had kidnapped my parents.

With that thought, Slurpinthal's house came into sight, and we stopped because it was time to put the whole plan into action. Time to begin this whole preposterous endeavor that I'd secretly dubbed the great Lawnmower Caper.

First off, we stopped for the lawnmower. Slurpinthal had a gizmo that he inserted at the top of our neighbor's machine, which quieted it and strengthened its power. Pretty nice attachment, right? I bet we could make big money off it, except, how would we explain it? Besides, we probably couldn't make more of them. Slurpinthal said that he'd made it here, on this planet, so it did have Earth parts, but . . .

We were wheeling the lawnmower forward. At least Clara and Slurpinthal were. I was kind of pushing with my mind, but I'm not sure how effective that was. It was hard to keep one part of my thoughts on my wheelchair and one part on a lawnmower. Besides, I was afraid I might push too hard and run over one of them. I wasn't sure about my powers yet. Did you hear that? Powers? Geez, I sounded like I thought I was Superman, or something.

We pushed the lawnmower toward the backyard. We were quiet like that cat we'd seen pushing through the reeds. Velvet feet. That's what Slurpinthal called it. He said we had to use our velvet feet.

Slurpinthal took off then, leaving us to sit and wait. He said he needed to wake up my parents. He had told me he was going to attach one of the gizmos in his pocket to the bars of the basement window. That way, when we pulled off the bars, they'd fall softly. Then my parents could climb through and escape.

Clara was holding my hand. She was gripping me so tightly, I wanted to pull my hand out of her grasp, but I understood her fear. What if something went wrong? What if the aliens discovered my parents were trying to escape? What would the aliens do to Mom and Dad, then?

A stray cat yowled in the night. It made Clara and me jump, but we didn't scream or cry out. We knew we had to be silent. This had to work. It just had to.

The screech owl cried out next. It sounded like it was at a distance from us, but we could tell from the sound of its screech that it was coming closer, hunting something. Did owls eat cats? I wondered, but, of course, I didn't speak that thought to Clara.

The moon was still glowing. It was low in the sky, so low it looked like we could almost reach out and touch it. I could see the dark patches that I assumed were craters. I didn't know much about the moon. I decided that when this was all over, I wanted to study up on it so I'd know what it was I saw.

Why didn't school teach you things you really needed to know? Why couldn't the schoolbooks tell you about the moon and about screech owls and whether their diet included cats? That was real information, stuff you needed a lot more than $3,572 - b = 2,688$ or the number of vertices on a rectangular prism.

Maybe, that's what Dad meant about reading and how it opened you up inside. I never understood that. I'd always thought that school was supposed to do the *vision expanding* as the principal once put it when he was lecturing us about studying. But school didn't do that, not on its own, anyhow.

I guess the biggest crack began from the desire inside us. We had to crack the zombie mode of our daily routine with a jab of curiosity. We needed to do our own *vision expanding.*

Little kids did that when they clung to dinosaurs, probing the lives of the T Rex, wondering about why dinosaurs died out, leaving the world for us mammals to take over. I remember when I used to read every book I could find in the library about dinosaurs, and I begged Dad to take me to the Natural History Museum in Los Angeles where they were going to have a "live dino" exhibit. (Yes, I knew that was all animated stuff, but still cool.)

But after the accident, I stopped exploring dinosaurs. I stopped doing that *vision-expanding thing.* If we survived this night, it was time to start expanding again. I wanted to know about moon craters, screech owls, the behavior of cats, and . . . aliens. I figured that would take me some time to read about, but after that, there was a whole world of knowledge I planned to scoop up.

Maybe one day I'd even add something of my own to that knowledge. On what subject I couldn't even imagine, but that was the exciting part about *vision expanding.* One thing led to another, and each dip into the research kind of zapped someone's brain into a higher mode.

(That's what Slurpinthal had told us when we'd sat around talking. Slurpinthal said our brains were like video games with a bunch of lights inside, and when we connected those lights by learning something new, we formed a whole new game. Then more and more lights lit up. Slurpinthal called it our individual Universe of Stars and said that each of us had that inside us.)

Suddenly, we heard a sound from inside the house. I was trying to identify it as to whether it was a toilet flushing, someone banging into something with their foot, or . . . A light switched on. Had we made too much noise? Had the aliens heard us? Were they coming out to investigate?

Clara's hand squeezed mine harder. I could see her lips moving. I thought at first that she was trying to say something to me, but then I realized she was praying. That was a good thing. I sent up a prayer, too: "Let my parents be okay," I said. "Please, let them be okay."

The light went out. The house closed itself back into silence. Only the screech owl on his rounds broke the stillness of the night then. Where was Slurpinthal? What was he doing?

The night was still sticky warm. It felt like summer. I started to wonder how I was going to spend my summer vacation. In the past, I'd gone away to camp. I'd learned to pitch a tent, to paddle a canoe, and to cook over an open fire.

Those were good things to know. Fun things. I remembered the hikes I'd taken through the forest, the pine smell, the squirrels chattering down at us. There were blue jays, of course. Lots of blue jays. Noisy ones who scolded and dived at us whenever we got near their young.

But there was no access for wheelchairs. Those trails were formed by crushed bark. I'd never be able to push the wheelchair down bark-compost trails. I supposed I could still paddle a canoe — if someone carried me out to the boat. I couldn't pitch a ball or a horseshoe. I couldn't climb a tree or dart in and out between trees, playing tag like we used to in the evenings. I wouldn't even be able to climb the steps into the mess hall where we went for meals.

"Someone's coming," Clara whispered, breaking into my thoughts.

The light went on in the house again. Another one followed. Had they heard Clara? It didn't matter because Slurpinthal was coming towards us, and Mom and Dad were with him.

Hurry, Slurpinthal said. *They're going to pursue.*

So we didn't get to reunite with our parents in a huge warm and friendly hug. Instead, I pulled Clara up onto my wheelchair, revved up my powers, and sent my method of transportation back toward the road.

I heard the others jogging behind me. We were all silent as the night sky. Apparently, Slurpinthal had warned my parents not to talk. Or maybe they were just saving their breath for the long hike back.

The road stretched out, smooth jogging, easy on the wheelchair wheels. We practically floated along. But then Slurpinthal pulled ahead of me and motioned that we needed to leave the easy route and strike off into the path around the creek. Before, I wouldn't have been able to go that way.

My parents flashed their hands. Stop. But I merely shrugged and then nodded at Slurpinthal. I turned my wheelchair and powered my mental connection higher. Clara clung, her eyes watching my parents, her lips smiling because they were with us.

We plunged into the darkness of the woods, a place where no moonlight streamed. It was all shadows and darkness. Trees stretched out their spiny hands to grab for us, their prongs scratching and piercing any skin they could touch. But the aliens were following, and a few pricks of fingers or arms were nothing to what they might do to us, so we jogged on into the night, hoping to get to Slurpinthal's shack and to safety.

When we finally reached our destination, I glanced back at Mom and Dad. Their faces were white with tension. Mom's lips had turned downward. They looked colorless. Her face had lines where I'd never seen lines before. Both parents had facial cracks and crevices, like our teacher, when she returned to school after being out sick with the flu.

Mom looked completely exhausted. I suspected that she hadn't slept well in the Slurpinthal's basement. Perhaps the smell of the mushrooms had affected her or the threats of the aliens. Her hand lay limply on Dad's shoulder, but I could see she was barely able to step over the entryway. The moment we made it inside, she started to collapse down onto the floor. Dad caught her and helped her sit.

He bent over her and spoke for a moment. Then he looked up and smiled shakily. "Clara, Kyle," he said then smiled again. Fatigue was written on his face as well. He looked older and almost as exhausted as Mom. I wanted to run to him, to lift him up and give him support, but I couldn't. I was wheelchair bound. What support could I offer?

"More comfortable downstairs," Slurpinthal said.

He had spoken, actually spoken out loud. Clara and I were so surprised, we blurted out in stereo, "You're speaking!"

The alien gave us a strange look, then shook his head as if he found us difficult to understand. But when he moved his head, it looked wrong, more owl twisting than human.

Somehow that odd movement reminded me of Charlie, a boy who attended school with us for a year before he moved away. Charlie had a large strawberry mark on his forehead. When you first met him, that's all you could see. The reddish growth almost glowed. It looked like Rudolph, the Reindeers' glowing nose, if the song had been about a real reindeer.

The strangest part about Charlie's strawberry mark, which he'd told us would one day disappear, probably by itself, is that after a week of seeing him, we didn't even notice the huge red mark on his forehead. We just saw Charlie, Charlie, the best batter on the team, Charlie, who knew his twelve tables, Charlie, who could draw a tree and make it look almost real.

Our teacher hung Charlie's drawings on the wall, and everyone wanted to draw trees just like Charlie did, but no one could. One day, he'll probably be a famous artist. I wonder if he'll still have the strawberry mark on his forehead.

I think about him sometimes. He was really popular at our school and not just because he was good in so many things, but because he was Charlie, a boy who was friendly and fun to be with.

Slurpinthal was like that. He'd first been an ALIEN, all weird and awkward, and then, when we found out he was on our side, he became Slurpinthal, the ally, and now, it was only at rare moments when his alienness appeared. Like Charlie, friendship overshadowed everything else.

Slurpinthal, unaware of my thoughts or ignoring them, turned his head around to the back, and motioned us to the stairway.

Clara ran to her mother, grabbed her, and said, "We have to go. You can sleep down in the basement. And there's food. Everything you need. We'll be safe, too."

Mom took Clara's hand and stood up. As I watched, it occurred to me that Mom really didn't look good. Her skin had a faint element of green to it. Had the aliens done something to her? Had Mom caught one of the alien diseases?

Dad took Mom's hand and kind of helped her to walk. My sister on one side, my dad on the other, the three moved like they were one unit. I rolled along behind them, feeling left out. Momentarily I thought about pushing forward. I could walk on Dad's other side, but then there was the staircase ahead of us.

I bit my lip and stayed behind. I didn't want my parents to view what I needed to do to get downstairs. Mostly, I didn't want them to see my fear.

I'd congratulated myself before on getting over my terror about *downleving*, but it was apparently a lie because my heart was once more beating louder than a freight train, and I felt the way Mom looked.

The three of them reached the stairs, and apparently, they were so tired they didn't even think about how I was going to make my way down. They stepped on the top stair and dragged themselves downward. Simple Simon.

Slurpinthal had gone first, then the others right behind him. I sat at the top, staring at the floor below me, wondering if I could do it again. Without a heave from Slurpinthal that threw me out into midair, my first downward movement was . . . well, a great leap of faith.

And then, just as if I'd chosen to begin, my wheelchair pushed itself off, and I found myself hovering in the center, about five inches above the top stair. I didn't stop to hesitate then. I just clicked into my mind and continued downward.

I knew that I could go from there. I'd done it before. I'd felt the connection with my chair, the cold metal, the weight of it, the way the chair slowly lowered, then stopped and waited for further direction on each and every step.

My parents and Clara were talking, I think. I couldn't hear their words, but Dad suddenly turned to look at me. His face paled even worse than Mom's. He stumbled then and almost fell, in his effort to turn and come save me from a fall. Mom clutched at his body, then twisted about to see what had gotten Dad all riled up.

She shouldn't have done that. It defeated me. I felt the immediate disconnect, a sharp ping as if a string had broken on a guitar. Except I was the string, and the wheelchair, out of control, tipped forward, and I fell.

Slurpinthal caught me. He opened his hands and absorbed my body, then stepped away so the chair didn't hit him. Except when I looked back to see the damage, I saw that the chair hadn't really fallen. It was upright, having landed squarely on its wheels.

Slurpinthal, the alien so small, he was hardly bigger than I was, carried me over to the chair and set me down in it. I think he saved my life.

"I lost control," I babbled. "I didn't mean to."

It is all right, he told me. *Proper control takes time.* Then he smiled. His teeth were orange and slightly crisscrossed. He needed braces — at least, if he were human, he would.

"Thank you," I said out loud.

You are welcome. It is merely what a friend does.

When the others, who had more or less frozen in place at the moment of my fall, finally reached us, Mom and Dad seemed normal again. They rushed over, hugged me, and Mom planted a thousand kisses across my face. It was yucky, yet at the same time, it was kind of nice.

Clara was right behind Mom and Dad. She pushed under and between and managed to crawl up into my lap. Then she threw her arms around my neck. For a moment I felt claustrophobic. But it was an okay kind of claustrophobia. I closed my eyes and waited for the flow of emotion to slow down. I felt like someone being pushed over by a series of ocean waves, half-drowning, half-laughing.

Eventually, Clara departed, Mom halted her weepy kisses, and Dad's pats on the shoulder came to an end. Then they drew back, and Mom said, "Are you okay? What were you thinking? How could you do something so . . . so . . ."

I nodded. "It's okay, Mom. Thanks to Slurpinthal. He taught me how to do it. Only my concentration slipped. But, he caught me."

I suppose they'd all seen that, but I'm not sure. Did they understand that something strange was going on with the wheelchair? Did they see that I'd been flying, so to speak?

A moment passed. My parents were sagging. Both of them this time. I don't think they were ready to study the weirdness that closely.

"Where are we?" Mom asked in a voice so weak and empty of expression that I blinked.

"It doesn't matter. Just as long as we're all safe," Dad said, staring at Slurpinthal, then sliding his eyes about the huge room. "We are safe, right?"

Slurpinthal gave one of his owlish nods. "Safe. Well locked. Food or sleep?" he asked.

Clara and I glanced at each other. Why was Slurpinthal back to his strange speech patterns? Why was he speaking out loud like . . .

Then, as if Clara and I had just come to the same conclusion, we nodded at each other. Slurpinthal was uneasy with my parents. He didn't know them like he knew us. He was being cautious.

"There's a really cool bed," I said, glancing at my mom again. She had collapsed into a chair, but the sag of her body was not normal.

"Could we have something to eat?" Dad asked, looking at Mom with the same kind of concern I was feeling. "Do you have enough?"

I suppose Dad was realizing that Slurpinthal was not the person he thought he was. Dad studied him for a moment, then glanced at me. I saw the question in his eyes. Was Dad at long last finally beginning to believe that Slurpinthal was an alien?

Chapter Thirteen:

Mom's Surprise

Slurpinthal moved away to get some food. He returned with a tray full of packaged items: granola bars, beef jerky, small containers of pudding, and juice boxes. He offered the whole collection to Mom. She took a juice and then hesitating, a granola bar and thanked Slurpinthal.

Dad chose a couple of beef jerkies, a granola bar, and a juice. Without a word he opened the drink and emptied it with a gulp. Then he started in on the jerky, chewing as he watched Mom, the same worried look on his face and lines across his brow that I'd never seen before.

Clara and I were hungry again. We took several handfuls from the tray and started unwrapping. I was just about to bite into my granola bar when Mom threw her hand over her mouth and said, "Bathroom."

Clara bolted up, took Mom's hand, and dragged her off.

"Another one," said Slurpinthal with a smile.

My head swiveled. I was trying to look at Dad and Slurpinthal at the same time, but my body no longer swiveled correctly. What was Slurpinthal talking about? Another what?

Dad was grinning. He understood. He nodded. His face started to look like it does after he has just delivered the punchline to a great joke and is now expecting everyone to break out into laughter.

Clara came back to us at a full gallop. "Mom's throwing up. Is she sick?"

Dad's eyes settled on his daughter, and he smiled. "No, Clara. She's not sick. She's going to have a baby. You're going to have a new little brother or sister."

Have you ever been in a windstorm that battered your face and body? You close your eyes because you're afraid the dust will blind you. Then you widen your stance, spreading out your legs so you don't fall over. As you feel the wind's force slapping against you, you think how much the wind is not only alive, but licking at you, nibbling at your skin. Maybe you think it's a beast trying to drag you off to its lair.

I don't know why I thought of such a situation. There was no wind in the basement. Perhaps it was because I'd closed my eyes since they were stinging. I certainly hadn't moved my legs. I couldn't. And the only touch of anything against my skin was a lonely tear cruising the pores of my face.

Mom was pregnant. She was having another child, another Clara, another boy, like me — the me before I'd gotten damaged. Were they replacing me? Were they trying to get a kid who was able-bodied, one who could walk, one that could help Dad with his vet work and have his clients all approve?

When Mom came back, Dad treated her as if she were made of glass. I'd noticed it before on our walk back from the basement, but then I'd thought it was only because of what they'd been through and how she was looking pale and unwell. Now I understood that this was something different. Mom was carrying his future son, the boy who was going to take the place I used to have.

Mom and Dad crept off — well, I suppose that's the wrong way to put it. It was me who felt like slinking off, not them. They simply

141

walked over to one of the holes that Slurpinthal caused to happen in the wall, and then they fit themselves inside. I'd never seen a sleeping hole from the outside. I was amazed when I saw them disappear after they folded themselves inside.

Clara cried out when she saw the wall kind of zipping closed. She ran to the place where Mom had been, but it was too late. Our parents were gone, or rather deep inside, behind the seamless wall.

Slurpinthal walked over to Clara, bent down (not much since she was only a little shorter than he was) and whispered something. I couldn't hear, but I figured he was just telling Clara that our parents were sleeping. I mean, we'd gone inside and come out. I didn't think the wall would just decide to eat people. It would burp them back out when they woke.

At least, I hoped that was true. I'll admit, seeing how they'd disappeared after our rescue of them was a little hard to take.

Whatever Slurpinthal said to Clara, she stopped crying, patted the wall where our parents had gone, and then returned to my side.

"What did he say?" I asked her. "What did he tell you?"

Clara gave me a strange look. She flipped her hair back from her face, tilted her head, and peered at me. "He was talking about you."

That was not what I'd expected to hear. Me? I wasn't the one who'd been eaten by a wall. Why would Slurpinthal talk about me?

Clara twisted her head back into normality. Then she scratched her nose, yawned, and finally opened her mouth. Quickly she shut it, and turned to see what Slurpinthal was doing.

"Clara, tell me. What did he say about me?"

Do you know how irritating it is when people do that kind of thing? I mean, they start to tell you something significant — or at least you think it might be something significant and important — and then they stop and forget all about it. Why is that? Why do they throw the hook into the water, the one with the wiggly worm, and then just forget that they were trying to catch a big fish with it.

Sometimes, they go off and read a book, or maybe they don't even bother to sit with the pole and the wiggly worm. Maybe they go swimming instead, freezing their limbs in the creek water until their teeth chatter and their skin turns blue. Then they come back to the pole and find that the worm is gone because some fish had gotten tired of waiting. He's dived down into the deep, probably laughing because he got the bait and didn't have to fight over it.

But here, in this picture, I was the worm, the poor wiggly worm who got eaten, and no one cared. Or maybe I was the fish still wondering why no one was at the other end of the hook, and how I've got a sore in my mouth because the hook ripped the inside of my mouth, and . . .

"Slurpinthal said I was supposed to be nice to you because you're hurting. That was silly. I'm always nice to you, aren't I?"

I shook my head, not because it wasn't true — mostly. It was because I was in the middle of a deep thought, fishing for ideas, so to speak, and Clara was talking about me being nice to her and about how I was hurt.

"What?" was all I could get out. "What are you talking about?"

Clara looked like she was going to start crying again. I decided she needed a nap, but then I turned and looked at the wall. Maybe it would be better if she didn't lie down in one of those holes, at least not until, well . . .

We must all get our rest, Slurpinthal said, coming up behind us. *I shall open our beds now. In the morning, we will talk. We will plan what to do. We must deal with them, I'm afraid. We can't put it off anymore. Besides, I want my house back.*

Okay, I was trying to process what had happened to my parents, my father's little announcement, what Clara meant, the fishing trip, and now dealing with bad aliens. It was too much.

"Slurpinthal, stop! We can't deal with the aliens. We've just gotten my parents back and now . . ."

Slurpinthal hadn't even turned around to look at me. He simply massaged the wall and opened up three new sunken chambers. And then, as if he hadn't heard me, he crawled inside one and lay down. In a moment, the wall, like a wave brushing over sand, swept both castle and moat into its liquid depths.

As the wall smoothed itself out, surrounding Slurpinthal, I turned to glance at my sister, but she was already sliding herself into the second capsule. I watched as she, too, disappeared.

The lights in the room began to dim. As my eyes scanned, I saw the machine that finds things slowly blinking out its colored lights one by one. Some of the yellow lights remained faintly lit, but no longer blinking.

The ceiling lights were also dimming, section by section. The machine continued its faint humming. I wondered if it ever stopped, ever slept, ever totally disconnected.

A great yawn hit me. I gave into it. My head felt weighty, but not with thoughts. I felt like I did when I'd stayed up too late watching a TV program that was way past my usual bedtime. I wondered what time it was. I wondered what day it was. I tried to calculate. I decided it was Sunday, and then I wheeled myself over to the remaining hole.

I had slept in that one before. It was the lowest of the holes, one at just the right height for me to lift out of my wheelchair and into its cave of a space.

The room was growing colder. I shivered. Then I pulled myself out of the chair, slid across, and onto the sleeping mat. I lay back against its softness, closed my eyes, and listened to the sounds. Was it ocean waves? Was that the rhythm of the crests and falls of pounding surf? I wiggled deeper into the mat, letting it ride me across the warm, liquid of the floating sensation of sleep.

***

My arm was numb when I woke up. You don't know how badly that frightened me. I thought for a moment that the paralysis of my lower parts was spreading into my upper body. My face was suddenly dripping with sweat. My heart half jumped out of my body. I couldn't breathe.

I didn't bolt up and scream, or anything. I more or less just lay there with a dull throb, a racing head, and a sad, sickness in my stomach. The thought "Why me?" scampered all about inside me like wild hares seeking safety from some sharp-toothed predator.

And then, when I came more fully awake, I finally realized that the numbness was only that my arm had gone to sleep. I'd merely slept on it wrong, robbing it of oxygen. The stabbing pains that hit me a moment later were welcome. They told me that my fears had been more panic than something real. My body wasn't getting worse. I was the same. I rubbed the arm and cracked a faint smile.

As I lay there, suppressing groans because the pain was beating against me, pounding warnings into my brain that I shouldn't sleep on top of my arm, I couldn't help wondering if my worries of the night before had been the cause of my morning panic. Had my fear been due to my disability? That didn't make sense.

The fact that I couldn't move my lower body was not something caused by a virus. It wasn't that my body had one morning woken up sick and been unable to move. I'd damaged my spinal cord when I fell. That couldn't spread to other parts of me, yet nightmares don't think. They just react. They make a single worry flare into something super big.

As my arm woke, still complaining with the familiar pricks and stings of limbs revving up, I felt reassured, relieved that what I'd most feared hadn't come true. The perspiration on my skin cooled. My heart settled into a more normal beat, and I was no longer gasping for breath.

I moved my arm, sliding it further away from me. It didn't like that. The throbbing increased. But it was good to feel the pain, good to know how false my nightmare had been. Even though my arm still hurt, my upper body was alive and well.

Without conscious thought, I strove to wiggle my toes, my legs, and my thighs. I sent the signal. My mind was willing, but somewhere, down beneath my waist, the signal short-circuited. I sighed. It wasn't that I hadn't expected that. I'd been trying that exact same experiment almost daily since the accident. You see, that signal used to work. It used to work so well, I hadn't even appreciated how simple it was.

That was how most people did it. Signal, movement. Kick, wiggle. Easy. But not now. Now there was nothing. No movement. No connection to my brain. Just a dull deadness. A limp nothing.

I sighed, a sigh so heavy and full of self-pity that it would have made a clown weep. The clown should, anyway. But nothing was any different that day or any other day. The constant injections, the visits to my doctors, the therapy — was any of it really helping? Why wasn't I feeling something in my legs? Why weren't they moving when I told them to?

My arm was better now, almost normal. It had feeling, life, and movement. So different from my legs, so very much the way it was supposed to be. So normal.

I closed my eyes and relived the nightmare. Have you ever seen flooding water? Perhaps it was only on a table or a counter where you'd spilled a pitcher of something. The liquid flowed, moving slowly after the energy of its fall. But it was simply water spreading.

The liquid had a mind of its own. It crept slowly forward, heading towards the floor. You could stand there watching the liquid, knowing that it would make a bigger mess in a minute when it reached the end of the table, when it spilled over. But just watching it was so mesmerizing you couldn't stop yourself.

(Mesmerizing is a word we learned last week in English class. It has something to do with the power of a magician. Mesmerizing is when the magician's mind has taken us under his spell, and we believe whatever he's trying to do and we can't look away.

Anyway, the water you're watching slowly slides its way across the table top, advancing like a liquid army of ants. You can't stop it unless you put a sponge in front. You could towel it dry. We do have the power to stop the advance of the water.

The paralysis of my dream was like that liquid water, except I couldn't stop it. I didn't have a sponge or a towel. In my dream, the paralysis just kept spreading, taking over. I was going to lose all ability to move, to be frozen inside a cask of bones and skin. A vegetable. Is there anything more hideous than a nightmare like that?

Maybe my worries of the night before were the seeds of that horror. Maybe one of those worry seeds had settled into my brain and sprouted thoughts of further body injury. Or was my nightmare just a coincidence? Even if I hadn't lain down full of dark thoughts, would

I have dreamed that horror? Would I have rolled on top of my arm and awakened in terror?

During the pain of my arm's reawakening, my bed hole opened. I think it responded to consciousness — or maybe to my eyes or the movement of my body. Anyway, I saw that the room was light. Then, I heard someone talking. Whispers. Were they talking about me? Were they saying how much a shame it was that I was disabled, crippled, only half here?

I slid myself to the edge of the sleeping hole, clasped the arm of my wheelchair, and slid out and down onto the chair with my new round, rubber legs. The chair groaned slightly. I wiggled into a more comfortable spot. It's not that I could feel a small indentation where I normally kept myself. It was my arms that demanded one location — and my head.

As I centered myself as always, I wondered why I always did that. What purpose did it serve? Would my lower body know the difference if I was perfectly in the center of the chair, or if I was closer to the chair's side panel? Would I look tilted?

It was time for a dump of my urine sack. My catheter was starting to itch — not a good sign. It meant I needed to sterilize the apparatus. I wheeled myself into the area we'd designated as the latrine and began to dismantle my own, personal, portable bathroom.

The first time I'd tried to do a hygiene cleaning, I'd thought "ick" and refused. But that was back when I wasn't used to it — back at the beginning of my fall from normality. Now, I hardly thought about it. Cleaning yourself was like brushing your teeth. It just had to be done. You couldn't spend energy on debating whether you were going to do it or not. Like your mouthful of teeth, the body demanded it. Ignore it, and it would punish you by erupting in pain.

Meanwhile, while I was taking care of business, my parents woke up. I found out later that it had been Clara and Slurpinthal I'd overheard talking. That meant that as I came out of the necessary room, I saw that I was the last to join the group.

"Kyle," Mom cried out softly. "Are you okay?" Her face held a secret smile. I'd have wondered about it if I didn't know what it meant. I could see that she was thinking about her replacement child, the normal one, the one that wouldn't have to spend twenty minutes cleaning a urine pouch and catheter.

I turned away and stared at the alien's location machine. I didn't answer my mother. I couldn't. My throat was feeling parched and scratchy. I attempted to clear it with a deep raspy cough, but that didn't help. I sounded like a car with a bad starter. That's me, a kid with a bad starter — legs and lower body that not only didn't start right, but never would.

Slurpinthal's eyes were peering into me. I didn't like the way his eyes made me feel. I shot a glance at him with a kind of warning — probably like the ones my dad used to give me when I was on the attitude brink, sliding down into trouble. My glare didn't faze Slurpinthal. He didn't look away. His eyes continued to inspect me as if, with his look, he was digging down through the layers of skin and deep down inside me.

Sleep has not yet cleared away your shadows? he shot into my mind with a mental voice that grated and itched. *There is an ugliness now that was not there before. You must purge this darkness,* he added, taking two steps closer.

I backed my wheelchair, but rammed up against the wall. My parents were on one side, Clara on the other. I had no retreat. Yet why should I need to do so? What did I fear from being in their midst?

I blinked, trying to escape Slurpinthal's eyes and the accusations in his mind speech. I felt guilty. I felt that I'd wronged somebody, but I hadn't. I'd only just woken up. What had I done to make him so angry? And what made me think that he was angry?

I had no idea what Slurpinthal was talking about. Shadows? Did he mean I had shadows under my eyes? Sure, I was ugly. I was a cripple. Of course, I was ugly. But why was he talking about it? Shouldn't he keep such thoughts to himself? I mean, I didn't go around talking about how ugly he was. And he had to admit his orangish skin wasn't all that attractive.

And what did "purge" mean? What was I supposed to be doing with my dark shadows?

I guess Slurpinthal saw my confusion. His eyes stopped boring into mine. He wiggled his eyebrows and then said, "We will eat soon." And off he went to scavenge for our breakfast.

When Slurpinthal came back with breakfast, he didn't look me in the eye. In fact, he avoided me, unless that was just my imagination in overtime.

Dad talked about what he and Mom had gone through, about how the aliens hadn't spoken much, but had let out that they were really after Slurpinthal. Dad told us that the aliens hadn't been mean to them, not really. They'd fed them and allowed my parents to be more or less on their own. The aliens had even gone back to our house and gotten a TV so my parents could watch the old movies that aired late at night.

But Dad was worried about being away from his work. You could see he hadn't enjoyed his captivity. He kept asking Slurpinthal when it would be safe to return to the house.

Mom, after her first babble about the horror of being kidnapped without a phone nearby so they could call the police for help, seemed to wind down almost immediately. She just sat quietly the rest of the time, with her hand across Dad's knee, her eyes on Clara mostly, smiling as if this were a holiday we were sharing with friends.

She did ask me a couple of questions, but I turned away each time. I couldn't talk to her. I couldn't speak without fear that I'd say what was really on my mind.

Stuffing a couple of warmed granola bars in my mouth, I acted like my mouth was too full to talk each time she spoke to me.

Clara made up for it. She talked and talked. She told them everything, at least from her side. Although I have to admit, she pretty much did say it all. That hurt, too. They didn't need a new kid. They had superkid Clara. Only five years old, but she could do it all.

Slurpinthal interrupted once or twice to add something he felt was important. The first time he spoke about how I'd given Clara rides on my wheelchair, letting her sleep in my arms. The second time, he told them how I was the one who figured out where the aliens were. But I wasn't sure that was true. Hadn't Clara been the one to mention the barred basement windows?

Clara got to the part about the lawnmower and stopped. "I told them not to steal, Daddy. I told them it was wrong."

Clara had tears streaming down her face over a stupid lawnmower. I shook my head. "We didn't steal it. We borrowed it. We did return it, remember?" I said and then stopped. I couldn't remember, suddenly, if we had returned the lawnmower or not. Was it still standing in the grassy area next to the basement window?

"It's okay, Clara," Mom said, sounding like she was tired again. "Sometimes you have to do something you wouldn't normally do. Sometimes — when there are people you love."

She was looking at me when she said that. I couldn't tell if she meant because I'd suggested taking the lawnmower to rescue them or because I was causing them to do things they wouldn't normally do. They wouldn't normally keep a crippled kid? Is that what she meant?

Slurpinthal was staring at me again. I turned my wheelchair and looked in another direction. Even so, my eyes glazed with tears. "I'm going for a walk," I said, hearing the anger in my voice, but not caring enough to tamp it down. Besides, what was there to say?

"You can't walk, silly," Clara said.

I heard my parents hushing her. Why? She was correct. I couldn't. I couldn't do anything. That didn't stop me, however. I fed my anger into the wheelchair and sped away, my hands stroking the rubber wheels so quickly the chair was in danger of tipping me over.

But I didn't care. The only thought I had was of freeing myself from my family and from Slurpinthal's eyes.

No one tried to stop me as I sped toward the staircase. I reached the bottom stair and prepared to click into the power Slurpinthal had shown me. But nothing clicked. Nothing happened no matter how much I gritted my teeth and wrinkled up my forehead.

Purity of mind, the alien said, walking up behind me. *Power has no fuel without it.*

The vagueness of Slurpinthal's words made my anger flare. I wanted to throw something at him. I wanted to invite the kidnappers to take the strange alien neighbor with them and to never return. I wanted that and all the things I couldn't do anymore — the life I used to have before I fell off my bike and ruined everything.

Experiences mold us. You are not the boy you left behind. You are someone else. Do you take that new path and form it into greatness, or do you waste yourself on pity?

I wheeled about with the rapidity of a basketball star on wheels. "Greatness?" I croaked out. "Who's ever been great in a wheelchair? Name one person."

The alien tilted his head. His eyes bobbled. His eyebrows twitched. I think he was laughing, but I wasn't sure. However, before I could get any madder, he said, "Governors, senators, attorneys, writers, actors and actresses, singers, musicians, teachers, presidents, scientists, . . ."

"All right! I get it. Like it doesn't matter, right? I can be anything — except I can't DO anything I want. I can't play baseball. I can't ride a bike. I can't . . ."

No one can do everything. But with practice or adaptation, we can do almost anything. Did you know there are hand cycles? They allow the hands to pedal. There are power bikes, wheelchair bikes, and many other adaptive cycles.

Dan Stevens is a man who has no legs. He plays in major league baseball, and he even pinch-hit for Daryl Strawberry. There are people in wheel chairs who compete in martial arts and wrestling. Did you know that there are wheelchair basketball, soccer, tennis, hockey, and football teams? Also in weight lifting, bowling, and ping pong. Practically every sport they want to. Swimming is a great activity. Pools have lifts and ramps to help people gain access to the water.

Slurpinthal sat down on the second stair. It didn't look right when he did that. His joints didn't fold like ours. I thought he'd topple over. But he didn't. He leaned back against the riser part of the stairs and exhaled as if he were sitting in a reclining chair, one padded and very comfortable. He stretched out his legs onto the step beneath him.

Confusion is in your eyes, Kyle. This situation has not given you this anguish. It was dwelling inside you. Just now it has bubbled up. It prevents you from rising to become. In the 1800's a man named

William Ernest Henley, after doctors had to cut off one his legs, wrote a poem called Invictus. He said, "I am the master of my fate, I am the captain of my soul."

Do you understand what that means, Kyle? That you determine what you want to achieve, no matter what misfortune life gives you.

I could hear the others talking. Clara was giggling. Dad laughed his usual snort of a laugh. A high-pitched "huh," followed by an indrawn gasp and then a couple of "ha-ha's." It was reassuring to know that some things didn't change. There might be a new baby, aliens attacking, secret powers, but some things just went on as if nothing else was different.

I'd said that the wheelchair didn't click when I turned the imaginary power switch, but just then I felt it. It was like the on switch was back. I knew how to take the wheelchair up again, but now I didn't need to.

"What president was in a wheelchair?" I demanded, thinking about what Slurpinthal had said.

He smiled. "Franklin D Roosevelt."

"Yeah? Name a scientist."

Stephen Hawking.

"I bet there aren't any artists or musicians, though. Right? Or movie stars. There can't be any movie stars . . ."

Christopher Reeve, best known for his acting in Superman, Itzhak Perlman, a famous violinist, and Frida Kahlo, a world-famous artist. King Phillip II of Spain. Helen Keller couldn't see or hear, and then became wheelchair bound. . . Do your homework, Kyle. Look these people up. Choose your heroes.

There will be many more in the future. Doctors, accountants, inventors, businessmen, CEO's of companies, judges, artists, musicians, teachers. . . And you, Kyle Green. Who will you become?

I wiped my eyes. Maybe Slurpinthal was right. Maybe I had been an idiot, feeling sorry for myself instead of learning about what I could do while wheelchair bound.

I turned to look back at my parents. Dad saw me and gestured for me to return. Mom looked up and smiled. Clara came running over.

Kyle, it's so cool," she said. "Mom says we're heroes, that we saved their lives."

A hero? Maybe I'd already started on that path. It was something to think about.

For the rest of the day, we talked. At first, Mom and Dad tried to get Slurpinthal over in a corner so "the adults" could discuss what to do next. Thankfully, Slurpinthal told my parents that we were all in this together and reminded them that it was my brilliant idea about the lawnmower that had gotten them out of their basement captivity.

Clara and I nodded, high-fived each other, then joined them.

Ideas gather within the brains of both young and old, Slurpinthal said.

I wasn't sure if my sister got that thought, but I smiled when I received it. It was nice to be treated as someone who could have good ideas. It was even nicer to feel like Slurpinthal thought I was important enough to include.

It was during that discussion that we finally found out about Slurpinthal. I mean, sure, Clara and I knew. We'd suspected it from the first. And all the weird things we'd seen him do had strengthened that belief.

But then, he came out and said it to my parents. "I come afar, Planet Threcia."

Of course, my dad burst out laughing. He thought Slurpinthal was joking.

Slurpinthal didn't argue with him. He simply allowed the orange of his skin to intensify. His ears sprouted spots. His lips changed their shape. His eyes expanded and grew more oval.

Dad was closest to Clara. He swept her into his arms. Mom gestured for me to come nearer, but I didn't. I shook my head and moved even closer to Slurpinthal.

"Slurpinthal is our friend," I said. "He isn't going to hurt us. Remember, he helped save you from the others."

Perhaps I shouldn't have reminded them about the other aliens. My parents' eyes jumped from Slurpinthal to me and back again.

"Why are you here on our planet? What do you want from us?" Dad asked, pushing Clara behind him.

Chapter Fourteen:

The Big Reveal

Dad was glaring at Slurpinthal, seeing him suddenly as an invader, as an alien who wanted to damage Earth or humans. I saw the dent in Dad's chin widen. It always did when Dad was at his angriest.

I moved even closer to Slurpinthal, bridging the small gap of space between us. Then I raised my hand and wished that I could place it on his shoulder. Still, it fell on his arm, and Slurpinthal turned to me with that odd lilt of his head that showed he was contemplating our human oddnesses.

"I am alien," he said, "but I do not do hurt. I wish friends, friendship." He stared down at me. He nodded, as I had done earlier. "This one I understand. He speaks inside. He bonds."

"Kyle, come here," my Dad barked out, but I shook my head.

"Don't you see, Dad. He's not going to hurt us. Listen to him. Hear what he has to say."

The cleft in Dad's chin deepened even more. His left eye started twitching. He was tired. I saw that in his eyes. No, beyond tired — exhausted. I glanced at Mom, afraid of what I'd see. She surprised me. Her eyes looked tired, too, but she wasn't angry. She was listening, thinking about what she'd observed and heard. She felt my eyes and smiled at me.

"Kyle is right, dear. I think Slurpinthal is not the enemy here. Who is? Who were the people who took us from our house? Can you explain that?"

Talk about a climax. We were there at that moment. All of us were holding our breaths, ready to hear what we'd been trying to figure out, what we needed to know. And then the machine burst into such a horrendous clamor, we froze, gasped, and turned to stare.

"What is it?" my father yelled. "Are they breaking in? Are they here?" As if it were the moment he'd been waiting for, he tossed Clara to Mom and sprang for me.

One of the worst things about being in a wheelchair is that when someone takes the handles of the chair in their hands, they can move you without regard to your wishes. I cried out against it, but I couldn't fight my father's strength. My hands dropped, and he pushed me forward, backed me, and then propelled me toward Mom and Clara.

And all that time, the machine blared a horrible noise – a bleating, atonal, madness of a sound, a booming beat that took away all concentration.

Slurpinthal subdued it somehow. It didn't stop, but the sound lessened. He turned to see what my father had done, for I think he'd only caught the idea of movement. The alien shook his head, then shrugged a half-hearted one-shoulder lift.

They fear what they do not know. I understand.

I knew exactly what Slurpinthal was referring to. My father had only wanted to protect me. It was something probably any parent would have done.

"What is the noise?" I asked Slurpinthal. "What does it mean?"

"They, the others, are here."

"Do you have weapons?" Dad demanded as if he'd suddenly forgotten that Slurpinthal was the one he didn't trust.

"No. No need. Safe. Can not enter."

I'm not sure that Dad trusted that, but I was positive that Slurpinthal didn't lie. However, I wondered if he really knew. How could he be so certain the aliens couldn't break in?

The ceiling thumped. The room shook. The lights went out, then blinked back on.

"Safe. Can not enter," Slurpinthal assured us. "More food? Drink?"

The thumping continued. The blinking lights, the bangs, and the shaking walls, and yet as Slurpinthal had promised, the aliens were unable to break through. We were all yawning and sagging against our chairs when the silence finally came.

Slurpinthal tilted his head and listened a moment. The machine's bleating had changed in pitch. Slurpinthal stood up, went over to the machine, and played with several knobs. In a moment, he stood straighter, turned around, and said, "They go. We sleep."

My mother was barely able to walk; she was so tired. My father was hardly energetic, but the two of them, without a whimper or a question, folded themselves inside the holes that Slurpinthal opened for them and lay back. Two seconds later, the wall covered them, and I saw Clara climbing into a lower hole as she demonstrated a very loud and rude yawn.

"You never told us about the others," I said. "Who are they? What do they want?"

Slurpinthal shook his head. *Your parents will not like this, Kyle. It will make them angry. The others have come for me. They wish to take me back, but I will not go. I do not wish to serve them anymore."*

I had figured out from things he'd said that the others were after Slurpinthal, but what did he mean to serve them? "Do they want you to do something horrible? Is that why you're running away?"

Slurpinthal turned to stare at me. His eyes bored into me once more as if he were searching for something. This time I didn't look away. I withstood the force of his eyes.

I do not run away. I escape.

To me, that meant the same thing, but when I questioned him further, Slurpinthal said that he had to "ponder it."

So I did what he suggested I do. I crawled into my hole and went to sleep. Sometimes when things don't make sense, sleep is the very best thing to do.

In the morning, Slurpinthal told us that he had decided to give himself to the others. I argued with him. I said that he shouldn't have to do something he didn't feel was right.

Turning sad, orange eyes toward me, Slurpinthal bobbed his ears and said, *Escape. Run away. They are the same.*

My parents were awake. Dad saw me talking to Slurpinthal and walked over. Apparently, even after we'd slept another night in the strange basement, eaten Slurpinthal's food once again, and been under his care for twenty-four hours or more, Dad still didn't trust the guy, just because he was an alien.

I mean, hadn't Dad always told me that people earned your trust through their deeds. Hadn't he always said that you should judge a person based on who he is, and not on the color of his skin or the way he talked differently than we might. Here was the perfect chance to prove that he really meant that.

I wanted to say those things to him, but I couldn't. You can't lecture your own dad.

160

Slurpinthal turned to stare up into the firm gaze of my father. He met that look, that look of distrust, and he nodded. "I go up. I show me. I go with."

"He's turning himself in," I explained to my dad. "He's going to go back to his world and be their slave again. He doesn't want to do that. He wants to stay with us. Tell him he shouldn't have to turn himself in. Tell him he should stay. Please, Dad."

I had pivoted around to plead better. Slurpinthal did not wait to hear what my father was going to say. He started to walk away.

I grabbed at Slurpinthal's shirt, holding him there. That stopped him. He turned, shook his head, and said, "Son persistent. Good thing this. But cannot stay. I go. I must."

"Why do they want you?" Dad asked as he disengaged my hand from Slurpinthal's shirt.

I heard Clara coming from behind. It was easy to recognize her step. She did a kind of skip-walk. Dad called it the waltz step, but it wasn't smooth like dancing. Clara's walk was graceless, tomboy written all over her — except for the fact that she usually clutched her doll in one hand.

"Slurpinthal says he's giving himself up to the others," I cried out, hoping that Clara would know the words to stop him.

Slurpinthal was staring at all of us now, for Mom had followed Clara. We were gathered around him in a circle, closing him in — some of us with tearful, pleading eyes, others with glares of suspicion.

"Slurpinthal knows what is best," my mother said, glancing over at my father.

Slurpinthal's head dropped. He studied his feet. As if there had been no span of time between Dad's question and the response,

Slurpinthal began to speak. "I ran away. Kyle told right. To run away is to hide. I hide away. Avoid responsibility. Bad."

He put his hand on my shoulder. I saw Dad take a step closer to me, but I was glad that Slurpinthal touched me. I wanted him to. I wanted him to be my friend, whether he was an alien or not.

But what do you owe them? Why do you feel responsible? I thought at Slurpinthal, hoping he'd catch my unspoken question.

His eyes met mine. "I am the leader. They elect me. I want not to be. I run away."

If I could have, I would have bolted up. I would have whirled around and said to my father, *See, he's a good man.* But of course, I couldn't. Instead, my mouth flew open, and I tried to organize my thoughts into words.

Clara beat me to it. "You're president?"

Slurpinthal looked down at his feet again. "Yes. But I not want."

My mother had come closer. She put her hand on Slurpinthal's shoulder. "Couldn't you say that you don't want to be president? Couldn't you remain here with us if you chose?"

My dad cleared his throat. Either he didn't like the suggestion, or he didn't like my mother touching an alien.

Slurpinthal looked up. "I say no want. They . . . they elect. No permit to leave the planet. They come. They take me home."

Dad cleared his throat again. He was going to say something, some platitude about how that was for the best.

Thankfully, Mom interrupted. "Is your presidency for a long time. Maybe you can return when it's finished?"

"For life," Slurpinthal said with the look of an alien who is doomed. If you can't imagine that, close your eyes and picture the way he once looked, his head held high, his ears snug against his body, not drooped and sagging as they were at this moment. His eyes had once been full and only pale orange. Now they looked pushed in somehow, and they flared with a vivid orangish-red.

Perhaps, I should say frankly that he looked sick, sick and tired, because it was obvious to even a person not of his race, that he'd had no rest the night before. I bet he'd spent all night thinking about whether he must go back.

The sight of him made me want to cry. I think I did a little. I know my cheeks felt wet. I swiped at them a couple of times and tried not to let the others know.

Perhaps there would have been more to the conversation then, but the machine suddenly started pounding out its horrible bleating noises of the day before. We threw our hands over our ears and watched as Slurpinthal rushed over to fiddle with the knobs.

"Now. I go," he said, as he lessened the noise and turned to face us. "Time."

I don't want you to go, I said, sending it in a mind wave or at least attempting to do so.

Slurpinthal returned to my side. *Some things are not escapable. We must adapt and do our best.*

I wished I'd never said that about escape and running away being the same thing. I wished I'd kept my mouth and thoughts to myself. Now they were going to take Slurpinthal away, Slurpinthal, my friend. And all the specialness in our lives would drain away. For both Slurpinthal and me. And Clara, too.

My eyes turned liquid again. I used my sleeve to hide it from the others.

The thumps on the building hadn't restarted, but the machine's lights continued to flicker off and on. Yet, inside the shack, we were all silent, solemn. It seemed more like a funeral procession than a walk to freedom.

Clara took Slurpinthal's hand. He was holding her doll. Had she given it to him to cheer him up? Would he take Babydoll to a faraway planet?

Clara was dragging her feet. She didn't want Slurpinthal to go. He'd been our anchor, our parent when our folks had been gone, and our only friend throughout this whole situation. Could we let him go? As if we had a choice.

Mom and Dad were holding onto each other. They seemed weak to me. Always before, they'd been rocks, mountains — perfect people, resistant to everything. Now they seemed faded. They were only human, after all. Not alien.

What was Slurpinthal's home world like? Did it have boys in wheelchairs?

As I sat at the bottom of the staircase, watching everyone climb, a thought plowed into my brain. What if I were to go with him? We could keep our friendship then. I could learn more about mind power. I could see things I'd never see on Earth.

Of course, I'd have to leave my parents and my sister. I would miss them. I wouldn't be here for the birth of my new brother or sister. But would they really notice I was gone? Would they care? Or would it be a relief? No more wheelchair boy, no more disabilities, hospital visits, and physical therapy.

Clara and Slurpinthal had reached the top. Mom and Dad were almost there, too. It was time for me to do the magic trick. I closed my eyes, found the click, and started up. This time my concentration was good.

I was worried about too many things I couldn't change, but I also kept the chunk of my mind that propelled me upwards strong. I was taking care of what I *could* control.

When I reached the top, Mom and Dad were too busy staring at the door to pay attention to me. I don't think they even noticed how I'd risen to the top of the staircase. Of course, maybe they no longer cared. The bitterness of that thought washed over me. I felt brittle, like parts of me were made of glass and one knock against my skin would cause me to shatter.

Slurpinthal looked back at me. *That is not true. You are strong, and they feel much love for you. You are their son — always, no matter what.*

He turned to face the outer door, stared at it a moment, and then looked back at me. *I would take you willingly to my planet, but I cannot. You are part of a family, a family that loves you. I cannot take you from that. It is not possible.*

He didn't turn around again to face the door, but it opened, and he walked through it, backward, his eyes saying goodbye to each of us.

As he took the fourth step, the door closed, the lights went out, and we were left standing there in a room as dark as the depths of the ocean.

Mom cried out. Dad swore. Clara began to cry. I pushed my wheelchair closer to the others, touched my sister, and pulled her close. Then I wheeled over to Mom. "In a minute, we can follow. He will be gone, and so will the others. Then we can go home."

Dad moved over to stand beside me. "Care to tell us how you got up the stairs, son?" he asked, whispering as if he thought the aliens might be outside listening.

I didn't know if I'd still have the power after Slurpinthal left, but my wheelchair connection was something I needed to keep a secret. It was a gift Slurpinthal had left me, a jewel. I needed to keep its warmth next to my heart. Perhaps it would take away my brittleness and the hardness that wanted to take over my soul.

So, I shook my head and reached out for my father's hand.

"I love you, Kyle," Dad said, still whispering as he shot a glance at the door. I think he feared that the aliens might burst through and attack us.

But just that hand covering mine and the words Dad had whispered to me changed everything. Slurpinthal had been right. We did form a family that cared about each other. Maybe my parents had some problems with my disabilities — or maybe it was just me thinking they might. Either way, as Slurpinthal had said, I was their son, and at that moment, with our hands entwined and our fear uniting us, we clicked as surely as the on/off switch in my brain that had allowed me to elevate my chair.

The four of us waited longer than perhaps we needed to. But when we finally opened the door and walked outside the shack, the area around the little building was deserted. Strangely there were no signs that it had ever been attacked, no signs that anything alien had occurred.

Behind us, the door clicked shut. Clara ran back to see if she could open it. When she couldn't, my father yanked at the door. But without Slurpinthal, we couldn't enter. The shack would be forevermore vacant.

We headed home. I didn't tell Dad that I could power my chair over rough ground. I let him push me along. Clara sat in my lap, clinging with her arms around my neck. My legs were probably asleep due to her weight, but it didn't matter. I couldn't feel it.

And when she got up, when the tingling that should have alerted me that the oxygen had been cut off from her weight on my legs, there wouldn't be any needles and pins because that part of me was dead. I knew it now. No matter what the doctors promised and Mom kept hoping.

The house needed some repairs from the rain blowing in. Otherwise, everything slid back as it had been before. Except at night, when I looked across to Slurpinthal's house and no lights lit up the room he'd occupied. The Simon's house was once again dark and still. No floating lights. No mystery. No alien neighbor.

Things at school went on just the same. Bullies pounced. Teachers demanded work. The intercom annoyed both teachers and students until you wanted to scream, "Shut up!"

And then, slowly, I began to see changes. Dad came home one evening and told us that he'd received a call to go to a new ranch where he'd treated an Arabian mare who'd snorted with spirit and pawed the ground in challenge even though she was sick. Dad knew right away what her problem was. He took care of her and gained a new client. The rancher told his friends, and soon Dad stopped looking glum as money started flowing into the budget.

Mom, much plumper in the belly, grew younger-looking. She got her hair cut, bought some new shoes, and began to smile. Last Saturday at dinner, right after Dad told a story about one of the goats he'd treated, Mom even cracked a joke.

Clara and I were so surprised by the miracle of that smile that we high-fived under the table. Mom telling jokes? Things went on like that for weeks, each one, in some way, making life steadily better.

On the Monday that followed that tiny miracle, Tom Sumpers caught up with me. He jerked my wheelchair around, gave me a lecture about how it wasn't safe to be by myself, and then tried to tip me over.

He probably would have succeeded, as usual, except that a patrol car just happened to be driving by. It flashed its lights, ran the siren, and pulled over to the side of the road. Of course, Tom Sumpers took off like a pack of wolves was after him, but the tall, skinny policeman jumped out of his black and white and ran like a track star. The policeman caught Tom by the collar of his shirt and slammed him onto the ground. He cuffed Tom, too.

The other policeman, Officer Mirf, took down my information and asked whether Tom had bothered me before. I told him the truth. Last I looked, Tom Sumpers was riding in the back of the patrol car on his way to the police station. I thought that was the end of it, but the officer called Dad and informed him about what had happened.

After his chat with the officer, Dad had a talk with me. When Dad realized I'd tried to tell him about the bullying but had only received platitudes about how I just needed to make friends with the boy, my father broke down and cried. "I never meant not to believe you, Kyle. I should have listened. I know you don't tell lies. Why did I think you were exaggerating about how Tom was treating you? I'm so sorry."

And then the following day, something that made my mom cry but made me cheer inside was when the doctor finally admitted that I wasn't improving. Oh, I wanted to hear that I'd be walking soon. I wanted the treatment to work, but I also wanted to hear the facts versus the wishes.

I'd been trying to wiggle my legs for six months, and I still couldn't budge even my small toe. No feeling. There should have been tingling, like when Clara sat in my lap and probably sent my legs to sleep.

After all the meds, the treatments, and the exercises, there should have been some kind of reaction to let me know things were improving. But there hadn't been, and I was pretty sure that none of it was working and never would.

So when the doctor finally called it quits, I didn't cry like Mom did. I just nodded my head as if I'd known, because I really had, you know. Besides, it was time to go forward from where I was, not from where I longed for it to be.

Like Slurpinthal had said, presidents, artists, musicians, and scientists could be wheelchair bound and still make an impact. I'd be like them. I'd make my mark somehow. I'd find a way to be special — a good kind of special.

I tried to explain that to Mom so she'd stop crying. But she didn't seem ready to hear that yet. The doctor patted me on the shoulder and said, "You've got an incredible young man here."

I think he only said that to cheer Mom up. I suppose it did somewhat because she smiled through her tears. Then she wiped them off and said, "How about some ice cream before you become president?"

Chapter Fifteen:

Moving On

Anyway, that meant that my weekly shots stopped, which meant that the physical therapist was no longer supposed to continue her treatments. She suggested that I should take up swimming. Mom gasped, but I smiled. I liked that idea. I wanted to swim. It was a place where mobile legs weren't mandatory.

Dad was enthusiastic about the idea, too. He dived into it, so to speak, right off. So it was he who agreed to take me for the special classes they offered at the public pool. That was a real relief because I knew that Mom would only have spent her time biting her nails and worrying that I'd drown.

Dad bought me a new swimsuit. He offered to help me into it, but of course, I told him that I could do that on my own. I placed my legs into the suit's leg holes and lifted up. My arms were strong, but it wasn't easy because I had to tug and lift, then tug some more. Truthfully, putting on the swimsuit was the second hardest part of swimming. The hardest part was trying to get my wetsuit off.

At least, that's what I decided later. But that first time, when I was unused to having the lifeguards lower me into the pool with their fancy machine, that was a little frightening. I was scared that they were going to drop me or that the mechanism of the lift might break. What if it got stuck in the middle of the process? What if the hydraulic motor failed? What if the straps securing me broke? What if I couldn't get back on the lift and was stuck inside the pool?

None of that happened. It was all smooth and easy. The lifeguards told me they had backups for everything, and even the motor had a hand crank in case the electricity went out. So my first hurdle was over before I knew it. And the lifting up out of the water, which they did so that I could relax before I attempted to swim, also relieved my stress over the process.

With those fears behind me, once I was in the water, I relaxed. The smell of the chlorine and the feel of the water took away my tension. Dad was right beside me, so I knew I wouldn't drown. At that point, I started enjoying it all, completely happy for the first time since my accident.

I already knew how to float. I'd learned how to swim before my accident, too — but that was when I had legs that could kick. Still, my swimming coach showed me how I could propel myself anywhere in the water merely by using my arms. I think Slurpinthal would have smiled to see me splashing about and floating like a lazy whale. In the water, I truly found freedom.

When we got home from the first swim and Mom found out that everything had gone well, she stopped stressing, too. As Slurpinthal had told me, we were all undergoing adaptation to each and everything that was new. Life was all about change and our attitude toward that change.

School ended, and summer began. Clara decided she wanted to go to camp, but I didn't. I wanted to spend my days reading and swimming at the public pool. I wanted to stay near the house, watching the kids play baseball.

Dad and Mom argued about my decision. They thought I should go to a special camp, one recommended by the physical therapist. Maybe I'd go there sometime, but I wasn't ready yet.

In the end, I got my wish to stay home. Dad let me help him in his veterinary work sometimes, and I did stuff with Mom around the house. I read lots, too, skimming the library for astronomy books and tales of aliens.

I was reading one of those books the night I heard a noise through my bedroom window. I got up and moved into my chair, then wheeled myself over so I could peer out into the night.

There was a light so bright in the sky it was like a raging fire, like the sun had suddenly appeared and was hanging over Slurpinthal's second-floor window. It was just like last time, like when he'd arrived that night.

The Welches' dog, the one that always barks, was once more strangely silent. The crickets and bull frogs stopped their chatter. The leaves in the trees even halted their swishing.

Leaning out the window, I saw the same bright light. Something started forming inside that ball of light. All the dots were dancing up, down, and sideways, and there was music — like a choir of angel voices singing Hallelujah.

Then I remembered how I'd gotten sunburned last time. I grabbed my baseball hat, jammed it down over half my face, and tipped my head so the light wouldn't scorch my skin. But I kept on watching. A man was forming in the light, a man just like before. A man I was sure was Slurpinthal.

Smiling, I wheeled my chair over to the bed and slid back in.

Welcome back, I shouted with all my might.

A moment passed. A moment in which I lay in that bed, scarcely breathing with my fingers crossed.

And then it came, a voice I'd heard in my mind so many times. *Finally*, he said. *They have voted me out. I am no longer president. Now I may do as I wish.*

Lying there, because it was just something I did each night from habit, I sent a signal down to my legs, telling them to move to the right. Of course nothing happened. It never did. But I didn't mind because I was listening to my friend, Slurpinthal, explain how he needed my help to work on a problem he was having with energy-birthing.

Of course, I had no idea what he meant, but that didn't matter. I fell asleep smiling.

Slurpinthal was back!